BEWITCHING BARGAINS

A Witch's Thrift Shop Mystery Book 2

ASTORIA WRIGHT

NOVELWRIGHT
PRESS, LLC

Cover Art by freepik
http://www.freepik.com

Published by Novelwright Press, LLC
http://www.novelwright.com

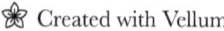 Created with Vellum

ONE

Missing Magical Persons

Witches and wizards weren't all warts and pointy hats. Nor were they bewitching beauties in ballgowns and tuxedos. They didn't live in candy houses in forests or castles in the clouds. Most of them— at least the ones in the city of Urbana, USA— resided in an apartment building hidden by magic. Aptly named Merlin's Shadow, the high-rise looked strangely normal both inside and out. Flowering plants by the doors and elevators and zen-inspired art in the lobby were not what Alice Adelcraft associated with witches and wizards.

Alice certainly never thought that she could pass for magical, with her frizzy, black hair, glasses, tan skin, and short frame not looking anything like the stereotype of a witch. But this wasn't the first time Alice had entered one of the hidden magic hotspots in Urbana. The last time she had been here in Merlin's Shadow, Alice had skipped the lobby and gone straight to the fourth floor—

broke into the residence of a jinn-keeper was more like it.

The memory triggered a reminder that there was a jinn— likely an angry one at the moment— with Alice now. Alice turned to see a black cat giving her a deadly stare on the other side of the glass door.

"Sorry," Alice opened the front door and let Naveed, her jinn in cat-form, into the building.

Alice still hadn't gotten used to having a jinn, or what most Untalented people called a genie. She also hadn't gotten used to thinking of herself as one of the Untalented, with a capital U, meaning *"You are not magical."* Alice knew she had no uncanny abilities, but the fact that anyone else did seemed like snobbery. Calling themselves "Talented" seemed snobbish at any rate.

Witches and wizards, collectively called Mages, spanned the world and the whole of human history but had only entered Alice's life a month ago. She'd stumbled into Magic Row, a street full of magical shops, and discovered the body of Naveed's previous owner.

That had led Alice on a witch— or wizard— hunt, as in trying to find the witch or wizard responsible for the dead witch she'd found. Alice probably shouldn't have gotten involved. Now, as she made her way up to the elevator to visit her new friends, she had to admit that she hadn't minded getting mixed-up in the magic community. Alice's involvement led her to become the master of a jinn in a lamp and a pretend-witch. She'd even discovered that her late father may have had wizard status, but his talents had clearly not passed to Alice.

Pretending to have talents, as magical abilities were called, wasn't easy. It might have been impossible without the jinn, Naveed. Alice took him with her whenever she was in the presence of the Talented. While Naveed posed as a cat, his magic allowed Alice to pose as a witch.

She started this morning by fooling Hazel and Zade. The teen girl and her twin wizard brother opened the door within seconds of the bell ringing. Their eager faces beamed nearly as bright as their blond hair. With a smile at Naveed, Alice was able to "manifest" two tickets to the World Cultures Museum in the palm of her hand without reaching into her purse for them.

Naveed yawned as if bored by his own magic. He wandered over to the sofa. Snuggling into the cushions, Naveed stared disinterestedly at the kid's reactions.

Zade grabbed one ticket with the exclamation, "Awesome!"

"This is perfect," Hazel said in a more even tone, taking the other ticket.

"What's perfect?" a male voice asked.

Officer Oberon Knight, Ron, as everyone called him, stepped out of the kitchen, tucking a notepad into the shirt-pocket of his Urbana PD uniform. Many witches would consider Ron the image of perfection. Tall, dark-skinned, and handsome, Ron was all muscle, confidence, and charisma —too much charm, as far as Alice was concerned.

The morning sun entered the living room window and shining across Ron's badge into his radiant green eyes. He looked smitten as he held the door open for

Liza, the twins' mother. Alice swore she saw more than friendly warmth between them.

"I feel so much better now that you're looking into it," Liza said.

"That's why we're here," Ron replied, gazing into her blue eyes.

Ron turned around, leading the way as he and Liza walked to the front door. He gave a wide grin to Hazel and Zade, his perfect teeth nearly sparkling as he said, "You guys have fun at your perfectly 'awesome' event today."

"We will," Zade said, holding up the ticket like a prize.

Ron stopped in the doorway and took hold of the ticket. He gave it a glance over and handed it back to Zade. "Mages on display for the Untalented? Now, I've seen everything," Ron said.

Hazel pointed to the title on her ticket. "It's just an art exhibit, see? 'Witchy Ways: A modern interpretation of urban magic.'"

"I'll have to check it out some other time, maybe with someone special," Ron said. Liza's fair skin turned the subtlest shade of pink to match her sweater. She was falling under his spell.

Ron didn't need magic to strike at the heart of single ladies. He wielded charm like a weapon, and he had practiced his aim on many a doe-eyed damsel. Liza Willows, with her blonde hair and hazel-green eyes, was as beautiful as any 'fair maiden,' as Ron liked to call them. Still, she was also four years his senior with two teen children and enough good sense not to fall for a heart-hunter like Ron. Alice had thought so, anyway.

Clearing her throat, Liza said, "Thank you, Officer Knight."

"Liza," Ron said as if chastising.

Liza's blush deepened. "Thanks, *Ron*."

Ron turned to the door and acknowledged Alice's existence for the first time that morning. "Oh, hey, Alice, I didn't see you there." Alice was short, but she wasn't hard to miss in her *green-as-a-leprechaun* raincoat. Ron flashed his dazzling smile—as if that made up for not noticing her— in exchange for a *"good morning"* from Alice. Then Ron disappeared— not out the door, just vanished. Alice would never get used to that.

With Ron gone, Alice might have commented on how his attention had been laser-focused—or wand-focused? —on Liza, but she wouldn't comment on her love life while Hazel and Zade were still in the room. Liza's attention switched to her children. She pulled the ticket from Zade's hand.

"Hey!" Zade said, now that he was clinging to nothing.

"Alice, you didn't tell me the topic was magic." Liza Willows, who was not just a single mother, but also a stressed-out palm reader at Reading and Co., looked like she couldn't take another problem today.

"Is that a problem?" Alice asked.

"The Untalented have nothing but bad to say about us," Liza said.

Zade reached for the ticket. "It's not like that, mom.

They're a group of witch and wizard artists pretending to be Untalented, pretending to be Talented."

As if that wasn't confusing, Alice thought.

Zade continued, "The Untalented think their artwork is meta…meta…"

"Metaphorical," Hazel said. She explained, "The group is really representing us so that more Untalented people will understand."

"I don't know. Blending in is one thing, but openly sharing about magic…" Liza let the sentence fall off her downturned lips.

Alice frowned. She should have realized that, aside from general distrust of the Untalented, Liza would have personal reasons to dislike Alice's choice for today's babysitting. Hazel and Zade's father was Untalented. The sting of him leaving them without a word or a way to sustain themselves would cause more than a little distrust of Untalented people. What Liza needed was for someone to show her that the Untalented were not all that bad. Alice hoped the exhibit would do just that, for Hazel and Zade if not for Liza.

"It'll be fine," Alice promised.

Liza glanced at her kids. She handed Zade's ticket back to him and said, "You win, but, Alice, please keep them in your sight."

Alice started to give the old scouts' symbol, then realized witches probably didn't have a scout's club—or maybe they had some witchy version of it—and changed it to a fingers-crossed promise. "Don't worry. I'll be with them, and so will Fluffy." Alice winked at Naveed, who had switched from the couch to the coffee table. He rolled his eyes and flipped a magazine page. Then he seemed to remember he was a cat and meowed.

"Aww, I think Fluffy wants our attention," Hazel said, looking at Naveed as Liza handed her and Zade their coats.

"Come here, boy," Zade said. With one arm into his blue and red checkered jacket, Zade picked up "Fluffy McScratchins," a.k.a. Naveed. Zade ran out the door, juggling a cat and fighting his coat to get his arm into the other sleeve.

"Bye, mom." Hazel finished buttoning her red jacket and followed.

With just the two adults left in the doorway, Alice asked, "Is something wrong?"

Now that Liza was a foot away, Alice noticed the redness around her eyes. Liza swiped her hair up, wrapping it into a bun and securing it with a band as she said, "You mean because Ron stopped by?"

"I wouldn't butt in, but it sounded like he was investigating something for you?" Alice said. Magical crimes weren't Alice business, but she hoped this wasn't something as serious as when Ron had questioned Alice about the dead witch. She asked, "Is—"

"Everything is fine." Liza seemed to read her mind. She continued, "It's not about us. It's about Mara."

Mara Blest. The name brought to mind the memory of a thin, nervous seeming woman with dark purple hair and lavender eyes. Alice met her once during Mara's shift at A Witch's Thrift shop. She's struck Alice as odd, but then so did everything in this new world.

"I only met her once at A Witch's Thrift shop. I think she quit the same day. I put in a good word for Hazel, I hope that's not what this is about, is it?" Alice asked.

"No, nothing like that. Hazel's interview is this afternoon, and she's excited, so thanks." Liza pulled the door shut and fiddled with her keys.

Alice raised an eyebrow. "Then what's wrong?"

Liza slid the key into the door, saying slowly, "I'm sure everyone knows I haven't been the best seer, but I have this gut feeling…"

The locked clicked. Liza looked toward her kids. They were already down the hall, pressing the elevator like it was a game of tag, and the button was "it." Alice walked with Liza in silence, waiting for her to resume.

A few seconds in, Liza said, "I had a vision. I know my talent has been off in the past, but it's been better lately. A couple days ago, I was looking into my crystal ball for a client, and I saw Mara's apartment instead. The place was littered with overturned furniture, books, and clothing. Ron went over there last night, and from what he said, my vision was accurate."

"What do you mean? Her apartment was ransacked?" Alice asked.

Liza nodded.

"Did you see how it happened?" Alice asked.

Liza shook her head. "My vision was after-the-fact. But this morning, when I woke up, I had a vision of Mara's face. I don't know if it was past or present, but Mara looked terrified. I had to call Ron and report it."

"Of course you did," Alice said. To anyone else,

Alice would have said she imagined it or that it was a dream. But Alice wouldn't say that to a seer— even one whose powers were on the fritz. Instead, she said, "Did you see who did it?"

"I wish I had," Liza said.

"I hope Mara didn't walk in on the thieves, " Alice said.

Liza shook her head. "You don't understand. I don't think they were thieves. I think Mara has been kidnapped."

Hazel and Zade had said that. Their mom had come to that conclusion even before her vision in the crystal ball, but Alice hadn't heard that theory from anyone else. She wasn't convinced.

She couldn't say anything else for now. They had reached Hazel and Zade at the elevator. Zade pressed a button immediately, despite Hazel trying to stop him. Unlike a standard, nonmagical elevator, the doors snapped shut before either twin could do anything about it.

Naveed meowed, but Alice shook her head no. Naveed didn't have time to stop the elevator with his magic, and even if he did, he was posing as an ordinary cat. Using magic would blow his cover.

Zade had just enough time to shout, "Oops! Sorry!"

Hazel simultaneously said, "See you downstairs!"

"Don't wander far!" Liza said, but the twins were already gone. She pushed the elevator buttons almost as many times as the children had.

"You might as well just wait," Alice said.

"You're right," Liza said. A moment later, her frustration pent up and ran down her eyes as tears.

"Liza?" Alice asked.

"They promised no more skipping school or wandering around Magic Row unsupervised," Liza said.

"They're just going to the lobby," Alice said.

Liza wiped her tears and sighed. "I'm sorry. I'm just worried. I made the mistake of telling Hazel and Zade my suspicions about Mara. I was hoping that they'd take it seriously and start listening to me about not sneaking out. But they've been secretive the last few days. I overheard them whispering last night about how they'll contact her."

"Who? Mara?" Alice asked.

"I hope not. I'm not sure. Hazel made up an excuse, and Zade said they were planning a surprise for me."

"How do you know they weren't?"

"They're teens," Liza said as she and Alice stepped onto the elevator, "Teens don't lie as well as they think they do. I just hope they don't try to go searching for Mara."

"I'll talk them out of it if I can," Alice said.

Liza shuddered. "Please do, because the way Mara looked in my vision this morning, she was terrified. Someone was chasing her, and whoever it was, I don't want them coming after my family."

TWO

Museum Mayhem

———————————

The World Cultures Museum mastered the art of minimalism. Wood floors, white walls, and a ceiling of hanging lights showcased canvases, sculptures, and artifacts representing the backgrounds of all the people of Urbana. Narrated tags allowed patrons to read about Urbana's history or press a button and listen to the text. Vibrant colors enchanted the eye, and a pin-drop silence stretched across the floor.

For Alice, the best part was the look on the kids' faces. It was part of the reason Alice had wanted to work here. Hazel wasn't the only one with an interview coming up. She'd rescheduled her own meeting with the museum's director for Monday—two days from now—and felt a mix of nervousness and awe as she walked through the museum.

She'd always felt that way here. Part of it was knowing that her father had been a curator here once. Having never known him, she could understand him better within these walls. Alice had only recently discovered that, in addition to being an archeology professor, her father had also been a wizard. Alice had not inherited his talent for magic, but she did share his love of history and world cultures.

Alice didn't know if Hazel and Zade had visited the World Cultures Museum before, but they were in awe of it now. Their excited grins made Alice's morning. Zade was a little overenthusiastic. He would have run ahead if not for Alice catching his jacket by the sleeve.

"Cool your jets," Alice said.

"My what?"

"Your broomstick," Alice reworded. *Did witches and wizards use broomsticks, or was that just a stereotype?*

Zade said, "Oh, yeah. I just want to get to the exhibit early enough to get an autograph."

"If we're the first ones there, maybe we can talk to the artists privately," Hazel said.

Hazel launched into a jog. Zade set Naveed on the floor and chased after her. Alice picked up her pace to keep up, almost tripping on the Naveed, who hissed in his cat form to show his displeasure.

"Sorry," Alice managed to mumble, before jolting ahead. "Hey, no running, you two!" Alice said. She caught hold of the twins' shoulders and pulled them both to a stop.

"Hey!" Zade said, yanking his jacket away from Alice's grip.

"Sorry," said Hazel.

Alice let go of Hazel's sleeve. "You're putting on quite a show." Several onlookers had turned their attention to the twins. Some shook their heads in disapproval. "Come on," Alice said.

She and the twins rounded the corner to an empty gallery. Thankfully, only one museum attendant followed behind them. She smiled at Alice and continued into the next room, not mentioning the running.

Alone with the kids, Alice said, "I knew you'd like the museum, but I didn't think you'd be this enthusiastic about it."

Zade asked his sister, "She doesn't know?"

Hazel said, "I didn't tell her, and you didn't tell her, so how would she know? Unless…Alice, why did you suggest we come here today?"

Alice didn't know what to reply. Not having an inkling of what they meant, she answered, "I just thought that it would be fun for you to see some art that mixes cultures because you're, you know…"

"Half-breeds?" Zade asked.

Hazel elbowed him and replied, "Our dad is an Untalented, but no. It's— he loved art as a hobby. He used to bring us here all the time. Dad's favorite artist was a woman named Belinda."

Alice took the pamphlet for today's event out of her purse, saying, "If she's showing her art today, do you want to go there first? Maybe she'd remember you."

Zade gave a wry smile. "Oh, she'll remember us. Dad was more than complimentary about her work when he thought magic was only bunk. He even discussed commissioning her to do a series of paintings for his offices. We invited her to dinner and everything."

He found his way to a bench and stared at a

painting of a red and yellow sky with one fierce black twister in the middle. In the middle was a man in a blazer, holding out his hands as if he had summoned the storm. It was called "Heartbreaker," and Alice pictured the Untalented Tom Willows as the man, if not the painter.

She sat beside Zade. "I'm sorry I brought it up. But, it sounds like a good memory. It's nice sometimes to relive happy moments."

"We aren't doing that." Hazel said, sitting on Zade's left.

"Yeah, it's not a great memory anyway, since the divorce happened a few months later," Zade said.

Alice squeezed his shoulder. "Just because something ends doesn't mean the good times never happened." Inspired by the atmosphere, Alice added, "We don't have to paint good moments over with all the bad ones that happen after. If we did that, we'd never have good memories."

"We're not." Hazel said. She took the metaphor and ran with it, "We're prepping a new canvas."

With a firm resolve, Zade nodded, "That's right. Today isn't about what happened. It's about what's going to happen."

Alice drew her eyebrows together. "What's going to happen?"

Hazel popped up from the bench. "Belinda is a friend of Dad's. She blended in so well with the Untalented community, our dad never knew she was a witch."

"Most Untalented don't recognize what we are," Zade said, adding, "It's like a secret identity."

Hazel said, "The point is, our dad hired Belinda to do a series of paintings for his new offices."

"She'd know where dad is and how to get in touch with him," Zade added.

"You don't know where he is?" Alice asked.

"When he moved, Dad said he needed some time to set up the new law firm and all before he'd contact us. That was a year ago."

"He still sends checks in the mail, but no return address. Nothing. He ghosted us," Zade said.

"Or he's in trouble like Mara is," Hazel said, with her hands on her hips.

Alice's heart dropped like a paint bucket from a broken scaffold— thanks to the scuffle she'd gotten into last month, she knew what that was like. Alice even knew what it was like to live without a parent or parents in her case. At least she hadn't also suffered an excruciating case of false-hope.

The kids thought they were going to find their father and convince him to come home. Alice couldn't blame them. But she knew from experience that wishing didn't make it so.

Thinking of wishes reminded Alice that her own genie had somehow disappeared from the conversation. Naveed— usually one to mock everyone's business and with even more skill somehow while in his cat form— must have strayed somewhere nearby. Alice stood, looking left and right without seeing him.

The museum might be pet-friendly, but Alice didn't think the caretakers would allow a lone cat on the loose. And Alice wouldn't be able to explain that he was really an impatient genie who took pleasure in losing his master. He was likely already in the next gallery ahead of them, where the exhibition was set to start in 10 minutes.

"Let's go on to the exhibit," Alice said. "But let me talk to Belinda about your father, will you?"

"What?" Zade asked.

"Why?" asked Hazel.

"Because she might not want to get involved in a family situation, but she'll definitely give a fellow witch the address of a lawyer who can help her with a legal matter."

"What did you do?" Zade asked.

Hazel smacked his shoulder. "She doesn't actually need legal advice. She's just pretending."

"Oh, right," Zade said.

"I'll explain in a day or two that it was just a misunderstanding. The exhibit is here all week," Alice said.

"And it's starting soon," Zade looked at his watch.

Alice, Hazel, and Zade heard a crescendo of voices as they entered the next room. The crowds around the exhibits made it hard to get a clear view of the artists whose paintings and sculptures were being unveiled. Hazel and Zade zig-zagged past patrons. Alice kept one eye on them and the other on the lookout for Naveed. But in the array of cats, dogs, and what was either a fur scarf or a ferret, the black cat-jinn was nowhere to be found.

She stretched her neck, glancing around until she saw that Hazel and Zade zeroing in on a tall, green-eyed woman. The woman stood out in her yellow, sunflower tunic-shirt and blue-jeans. With graying brown hair and a soul-felt smile, the woman looked like a friendly sort of person.

Alice tapped Hazel's and Zade's shoulders, saying, "Why don't you guys look at another exhibit?"

Zade opened his mouth to argue, but Hazel grabbed his hand, and the two changed direction. Alice, trying for incognito, took a slow route past a few paintings before making her way to the artist in question. When she came to Belinda's exhibit, she realized Belinda was not a painter at all, but a photographer. What was more, her wall featured photographs taken all around Magic Row. They were angled in such ways that they did not reveal specific locations, but anyone who had been there would recognize the street.

One picture captured a view of the road as a whole filled with witches and wizards during what must have been a celebration. Orbs floated in the air and all around the people in the picture, perhaps a luminary display they had all cast with their wands. Another photo featured Hex, the cat protector of Magic Row, her golden eyes glowing as she stared directly into the camera lens. A whole series of snapshots taken in sequence displayed the inside of A Witch's Thrift Shop in the midst of an inventory stocking, as the objects sorted themselves midair onto the shelves. Every scene was magic, captured in action.

Belinda chatted with a middle-aged man in a grey sweater and jeans, who slid his glasses to the tip of his nose to examine the pictures. He commented on the digital "tricks of light" that produced the "special effects," giving the "illusion of magic." If it had all been tricks instead of real magic caught on tape, the pictures would have made a masterful display of creativity. Even knowing magic was involved, Alice was impressed at the beauty of the angles and lighting.

"Absolutely astonishing," the man said, then he left to study another display. Alice read the name on the bottom of the photographs as she walked up to the artist, just to be sure she had the right person. Belinda Witcher, it read.

Witcher seemed on the nose for a last name of a witch pretending to be a regular woman pretending to be a witch. Wasn't that a mind-game! But only Alice and a handful of others in the room knew the patrons were being fooled.

"Belinda?" Alice asked.

"Yes?" Belinda replied, extending a hand.

Alice took it, saying, "I'm Alice Adelcraft."

"Glad to meet you, Alice." Belinda's grip was firm.

"Likewise," Alice said. Then, she leaned forward, adding in a hushed voice, "Always glad to meet another Talented person."

A mischievous twinkle in Belinda's eyes added to her smile. "Well, likewise on that. I haven't seen you in the community before?" She asked it like a question.

Alice answered, "I'm new in town. Actually, I'm new to everything in the community. If you know any good doctors, lawyers, accountants, anything like that, you have to let me know."

"Will do," Belinda said.

Alice shifted her eyes to the paintings, pretending to

study them, "These are wonderful. They remind me of a collection I saw recently in town. Somewhere in someone's office." She put her hand to her chin, hoping her acting was believable.

"I do have a collection in an office complex in town," Belinda said.

Alice snapped her fingers. It was too far. Who literally snapped their fingers when they remembered something? Still, she had to go with it. "That's right, I remember now. It was a lawyer's office. A good one, too. I wish I remembered his name, if I'd known he had any ties to our community, I'd have gone with him," Alice said.

"You're looking for a criminal lawyer?" Belinda asked.

Alice's nervousness turned to dread. Criminal? Alice hadn't thought about what type of lawyer Tom Willows might have been. Alice's reputation in Magic Row would change from witch to warlock, a breaker of magic law if she made another misstep. Alice tried keeping her calm as she replied, "Yes, well, it's just a misunderstanding." She cringed internally, fighting the wince that appeared on her face.

Belinda said, "Tom is a great choice for criminal law. He's never had a case where the charges weren't dropped or the sentence heavily reduced. Once he made the plaintiff pay for a defendant's injury while trespassing on his property."

"Impressive. That's Tom …let's see Wilson, right? I can't remember his last name."

"Willows," Belinda said. She took out a card-case

and flipped to find one with a WW in gold and black. It almost looked like a credit card. Although the slot seemed thin enough to only carry one card, when Belinda took the card out, another appeared beneath it. Belinda handed the card to Alice. "It's Willows and Westinghouse Criminal Law Attorneys," Belinda said.

"Thanks."

Belinda smiled. "I'm sure he's just the person you're looking to find. His ex-wife and kids are Talented. But then I'm guessing you already knew that." Belinda turned her eyes toward a pair of teens who snapped their heads away, pretending to be interested in the Magic of Music exhibit. Zade picked up a kazoo to add to the ruse.

Alice let a breath escape her lips. "They just want to see him. He doesn't have to talk to his wife or see any mages or have anything to do with magic. Those kids need their father."

Belinda looked between Alice and the two kids. They had given up their ruse entirely and were openly staring at her from the other side of the room. Belinda's expression changed. "Tom doesn't hate mages, he knows I'm a witch, he's even done business with us sometimes. It's just...he felt deceived, and I think if he's honest— it scared him at first to even know we exist."

Alice nodded. She understood how scary the idea of magic, real magic, existing could be to an Untalented. She herself had stumbled upon Magic Row in the worst way when she found a hexed dead body by a dumpster.

Belinda continued, "Even if he wants to see them, I heard his ex and her kids moved into Merlin's Shadow.

If you really are new here, you might not know: The Untalented are not allowed in hidden places like that. Tom is, naturally, scared of the threat of getting hexed for setting foot on mage territory."

"Well, there is that." Alice chuckled, not because it was funny, but because she would be in the same danger if anyone on Magic Row knew she wasn't a witch. "But it can't just be the hex keeping him away. He could write a letter. He could meet them outside of Merlin's Shadow."

"I honestly think he wants to see them, even if he had to go to Merlin's Shadow or Magic Row to do it. He just doesn't know how to swallow his pride and make the first move. He thinks they're just fine without him."

"They're not," Alice said in a matter-of-fact tone. "Will you tell him…"

Belinda held a hand up and shook her head. "I have tried, as his friend. But he's not going to listen to me. He needs to hear it from them." Belinda looked over at the children.

Alice wasn't sure she wanted to put the kids through that. A man not seeing his children because of pride? Alice couldn't understand it and wasn't willing to risk the kids' mental health for such a man to have a second chance at rejecting them.

"If they reached out and asked him to meet, would he go?" Alice asked.

Belinda said, "Yes, I think so." Belinda looked down, breaking eye contact.

"What is it?" Alice asked.

Looking back at Alice, Belinda said, "I know I

shouldn't have, but I enchanted one of Tom's business cards a while back to grant him entry to Magic Row. I had hoped he'd use it to see Liza, to learn about us so he could make it work between them. I don't think he ever used it."

"He was scared of the hex, and rightly so. I don't blame him for not using the card," Alice said.

Belinda waved a hand, dismissing the idea. "I've never seen the hex used. It's not like anyone's checking for Untalented since they can't get in without magical help anyway. It'd be easy enough to say he's from out of town or new to the area when people ask him questions."

Alice didn't argue. She hoped Belinda wasn't putting two and two together to realize that Alice was "new in town" the same way Tom might claim. The threat Belinda seemed to think didn't exist was all too real. Celeste Bellamy, the owner of A Witch's Thrift Shop, had called Alice out as Untalented within minutes of meeting her. Thankfully, Celeste had agreed to keep Alice's secret, but others would hex Alice in a second. She couldn't put Tom in that kind of danger. Alice reached for the card.

"May I take this to Liza? It might be better for her to meet him outside of Magic Row," Alice asked.

Belinda handed her the business card. Alice gave her a heartfelt, "Thank you."

Belinda smiled. "I only ever wanted to help." Belinda gave a sidelong glance at Hazel and Zade as she added, "Tom wasn't ready to talk to Liza or the kids before. I hope he's ready now."

The twins met Alice before she was five steps away from Belinda, immediately inquiring how it went. Alice tried shushing them and moving them along to the next exhibit, but Zade blocked the path with both hands out.

"She gave you something," Zade said.

"Relax. It was just a card." Alice slid the business card into her purse and kept her voice low.

"Is it Dad's card? Do you know where he is? What did Belinda say?" Zade asked all three questions in one breath.

After a moment's hesitation, Alice said, "I might be able to contact him. But even if I do, I can't make any promises that he'll come and meet you. Now, don't you want to see the rest of the exhibits?"

"I don't think we can," Hazel said, though the way it came out, it sounded like "I don't believe it!" Hazel was looking directly past Zade's head.

A woman in pearls and a pink sweater dress standing nearby looked where Hazel was looking. She held her hand up to her mouth. Her exclamation of "Oh my!" caught the attention of several patrons and prompted more than a few gasps.

Alice looked up. An artist in the midst of unveiling his wall-length mural dropped the canvas' covering and nearly fell from the ladder. The source of his shock was a simple word, Freak, smudged in bright red paint atop his "Portrait of a Witch." The image of a woman with raven black hair smiled out of the painting with a mustache and blacked-out teeth. Unless the artist was a jokester, this was not the masterpiece he'd painted.

The artist's horrified expression had dissolved into

tears. Belinda rushed over to comfort him. Several of the other artists uncovered their exhibits to the same type of surprise.

"Who would do this?" Hazel's jaw dropped, and her hands cupped her face in an imitation of Edvard Munch's "The Scream."

"Someone who knows how to break into high-security places," Zade said.

"Someone with a trickster personality and the magic to make the paint dry under wraps," Hazel said.

Hazel and Zade looked at each other. "Puck!" They said in sync.

Hazel shook her head. "What are we thinking? Puck only plays tricks on people for food or money."

Zade nodded. "And he doesn't make fun of witches and wizards. He wouldn't do this. Right Alice?"

Hazel and Zade looked at Alice, but she wasn't looking at them. Alice turned her head left and right. She searched over the whole of the crowd and began walking.

"Alice?" Zade asked as he and Hazel followed.

"Come on," Alice said, still walking at a fast enough pace that the twins had to hurry to keep up.

"Why are you going?" Zade asked.

"Is something wrong?" Hazel asked.

Yes. Something was very, very wrong. Alice didn't want to frighten the children, but to keep from panicking herself, she had to ask in an even and steady voice, "Have either of you seen my cat?"

THREE

Street Magic

T he cat-jinn was not inside the museum. Alice called out three times in her mind for Naveed to come back. Even though thinking his name did have some kind of power Alice didn't understand, *wishes* had to be said aloud.

Alice waited until she, Hazel, and Zade were outside. Then she whispered, "I wish you'd show yourself, Naveed," in a low enough voice she hoped the twins didn't hear.

Hazel and Zade were busy calling out, "Here, Fluffy!" Some spectators noticed the commotion. They asked the twins questions like, "What color is your cat?" and "Where did you last see him, hon?"

Alice thought she heard a meow. Instinctively, her eye was drawn to a crowd gathering on the side of the museum. She kept the twins in view but walked closer to the action.

Somehow, it didn't surprise Alice to see the 15-year-old street urchin, Puck, at the center of the crowd. He wore a magician's top-hat over his wild red hair and a maroon sweatshirt and jeans that did not complete the look. A makeshift table had been made out of an upside-down cardboard box with a red blanket hanging not quite far enough over it. A variety of objects sat atop the cloth: a deck of cards, a stack of cups, and other things one might expect of a street magician.

"Everybody gets a look. Nothing in my hat, right? Wrong." Puck flicked the top-hat three feet above his head. He caught the hat by the rim, which — to the amazement of the crowd— became the launching point for somersaulting black cat.

Naveed rolled onto the pavement and landed at Alice's feet. Seeing Alice with her arms crossed above his head, Naveed blinked five times, then disappeared. The crowd gasped, gaping at the empty space where the black cat had been. Puck set the hat down quicker than Naveed had tumbled out of it.

"Uh, Ta-da! Ladies and gentlemen, that was my *Magical Disappearing Cat Act*." Puck took a long, deep bow.

The audience broke into cheers and laughter. Puck wiped the sweat from his forehead and waited for the applause to die down, then he wrapped it up quickly with, "That's it, everyone. Tips are appreciated; just leave them on the table. Thank you, and have a nice day!"

A few of the spectators gave Puck a dollar or two and their compliments. Puck pocketed the money and folded everything else into the red handkerchief. He tried to make a run for it, but Alice blocked him. She crossed her arms and gave him her sternest look.

Puck clicked his fingers, and the tablecloth disappeared into his hat. He saluted Alice, giving her a mischievous grin. Then, he put the cap on his head and began to disappear.

"Oh, no, you don't." Alice grabbed his sleeve, and Puck reappeared. An old man stepped up to the boy. Alice let go of Puck, not wanting to cause a scene.

"You have the makings of a real magician," the man said.

Puck turned white. Alice noticed now, too, that it was not just an Untalented spectator giving Puck more praise. The old man was the only level ten wizard in Urbana.

"Rhys?" Alice asked.

Rhys Merlin took a sip from his Styrofoam cup, not saying a word. All he had to do was raise one eyebrow. Puck full-on panicked.

"You're not going to report me, are you? I wasn't doing any harm! Those Untalented had no idea that I'm—"

"Puck!" Hazel interrupted.

Zade ran forward. "Stop talking! You'll only make it worse."

Rhys lowered his cup, to reveal a grin that gave Alice chills. "Do you know why the rule exists that Talented people cannot perform magic in front of the Untalented?" Rhys asked.

Puck reddened, saying, more softly this time, "I

didn't reveal that magic exists. They thought I was an illusionist."

Rhys's smile vanished. He said, "Illusionists only pretend to do what we can do. The Untalented need to be able to figure out how you are doing your magic, or eventually they'll realize that it *is* magic and not an illusion at all. If you do enough of these street shows, they'll put two and two together."

Hazel said, "You should be careful."

"They're Untalented, not dumb," Zade added.

Puck replied, "I'm not stupid either. I didn't do any magic that an Untalented couldn't pretend to do with one of their tricks."

"The cat disappeared!" Zade said.

"Out of thin air," Rhys added.

"I didn't do that!" Puck said. His eyes flicked toward Alice.

Now all of them were looking at Alice, and Naveed was still nowhere in sight. How had Alice thought having a genie would help her blend into the magic community? So far this morning, he was only getting her in trouble.

Alice tried for an innocent shrug, saying, "I guess it was instinct."

"Yours or the cat's?" Rhys asked.

"Your cat is a magic one like Hex?" Hazel asked.

"That's so cool!" Zade said, looking around now for Naveed.

Alice might have said yes, except the way Rhys was staring unnerved her. Alice had a feeling magical cats were not a real thing. Rhys and the very few level ten mages in existence must have known genies could take on any form, including black cats. Alice couldn't reveal he was a jinn, so she didn't say anything.

"Am I in trouble, sir?" Puck asked.

Rhys turned his unsettling stare toward Puck. He leaned closer to Puck's face. "I think you ought to find the lady's cat. And take this as a lesson and a warning: People don't love what they fear, and the Untalented fear nothing more than magic. The same ones who will applaud the illusion of magic will take their pitchforks to the reality of it. Don't give them a reason to believe."

Alice's jaw fell. Rhys walked to the dumpster and discarded both his coffee cup and the conversation. But Alice wasn't about to let him go on that note.

"Kids, go wait at the bus stop. Stay where I can see you," Alice said.

"But—" Hazel began.

Alice narrowed her eyes, "Now or I won't treat you to lunch at Readings."

Zade took hold of his sister's coat sleeve, replying to Alice. "You don't have to tell me twice. Can Puck come, too?"

"Yes, as soon as he finds my cat," Alice said over her shoulder as she caught up with Rhys.

"Fine," Puck said, taking off the top hat and making it disappear. He pulled the hood of his sweatshirt over his head and stuck his hands in his pockets, vanishing in full view as he walked away.

Rhys shook his head. "That boy won't ever learn to hide his magic."

Alice balled her fists. "I get that you hide your magic

from the Untalented, but' pitchforks?' What century do you think this is?"

Rhys seemed surprised, but he answered with a shrug. "The weapons may not be the same, but the danger is as real now as it was in the past."

"No, it's not. We're not the same people we were before."

"We?" Rhys asked.

Alice froze. Rhys knew her mother wasn't a witch; what if he suspected she didn't inherit her father's magic? If he found out that Alice was Untalented... Alice shuddered as she imagined the hex mages used on the Untalented who made their way into Magic Row: A complete memory wipe.

She rethought her answer. "Yes, *we*. All of us, Talented and Untalented, have learned to be better. Haven't we?"

"Hmm." Rhys said.

"Hmm, what? Does that mean you agree with me, or you're thinking about it?"

Rhys lifted his chin to gesture ahead of him. "It means the bus is here."

Alice turned to see the doors of the bus opening, she nodded at Hazel and Zade for them to get on. Then she turned back to Rhys. "All I meant was that I hope you'll think about what you say to Puck. It's a dangerous message to send that the Untalented won't accept him because he's different." Alice left him with those words, heading toward the bus.

Just as she reached the open doors, Rhys appeared

in front of her. He held an open palm toward the inside of the bus. Rhys was smiling beneath his beard.

"You are brave, Alice."

"Thank you," Alice said.

"Brave is only a compliment depending on the situation. Telling an old man like it is, is brave." Rhys turned his back on Alice as she got on the bus, getting in one last remark: "Not heeding his advice is stupid."

FOUR

Reading & Co. Bookstore

R eading and Co. was unique among bookstores. Customers entered through a café with blue walls covered in art by local artists. Glass panels displayed baked goods and sandwiches of nearly every variety, which refilled themselves whenever one was taken. The espresso and other coffee machines had a silvery shine. Best of all, the scent of fresh-brewed everything mixed in heavy aromas one could almost taste through the air.

To the left, a room with large windows and galaxy-print curtains invited patrons to have their palms read for only $25, get a tarot reading for $50, or see their immediate futures via crystal ball starting at a $100 for a year-ahead forecast.

Past the café and Reading Room, the bookstore boasted titles from *Alteration Spells* to *Zapping Away Your Troubles* on shelves that looked more like tree branches growing along the walls. Reading areas with sofas, tables, and even meditation chairs sat in clusters spread across the shop. At a round table just past the café to the right, a writers' group was currently discussing how to accurately write Untalented characters. Just behind the Reading Room to the left, an art teacher instructed three teen witches, and one teen wizard used their wands to paint. Alice couldn't see what they were painting, but it was impressive enough to see globs of paint float through the air toward the canvas.

Most eye-catching, however, was a woman in a red dress who looked like she'd stepped out of a work of art. She was just exiting the reading room, with a red leather bag and matching hat in her hands. Alice instinctively identified her as Titania Knight.

Alice couldn't say that the rumors of Titania's beauty were exaggerated. She was a walking hourglass, thin but curvy at all the right angles. Her sandy skin glistened even in the dim light of the café. She must be radioactive in sunlight, Alice thought, imagining Titania with a literal glow around her.

Titania flicked her long, light-brown hair off her shoulder, put on her hat and sunglasses, and took one step before stopping. Sliding her sunglasses down her nose, Titania looked directly at Alice.

Alice, standing in line at the counter with the twins, looked away. She was self-conscious enough, with her short frame, curly hair, and glasses. She didn't need anyone giving her a once-over, sizing Alice up as Titania was doing now. Instead of flashing the condescending smirk Alice was expecting— and probably deserved since she had been judging Titania a second ago— Titania seemed upset. She hid watery eyes behind her shades and walked to a front table, where she sat with her back to Alice. Alice watched her stare out the window, wondered what had her near tears.

"There's mom," Hazel said.

Liza came out of the Reading Room, rubbing her left temple and hiding her weariness. She gave her kids an attempt at a smile.

"Back early? How was the museum?" Liza asked.

"Good." Hazel's smile was as fake as the one on her mother's face.

Zade straight-out sulked. "It was OK."

Alice gave Hazel a $20 bill, saying, "Get a sandwich of the day for me, please?"

"One for me, too," Liza said.

Hazel nodded, and she and Zade went to the counter. Alice and Liza walked to a table far enough from Titania's seat for Alice to ask without being over-heard, "What happened in Titania's reading today that made her so upset?"

Liza tried nonchalance. "What makes you think she was unhappy?"

Alice called her bluff, looking directly at Titania. True, Titania couldn't sulk with her princess-straight posture, but she was staring out the window, motionless.

Liza frowned. "I can't talk about my clients' read-ings. It's confidential."

"OK. Then what's upsetting you? Did you find something out about Mara?"

"No." Liza glanced at her kids and back to Alice. Leaning forward, she said, "My bad feeling is worsening, Alice. I'd say it was a premonition, but you know my talent hasn't been consistent."

"You said it was getting better," Alice reminded her, though she still wasn't sure she believed it.

"Well, Celeste doesn't seem to think so," Liza said.

"She still thinks Mara just quit?" Alice had to admit she agreed. She hadn't wanted to discount Liza or the kids. Still, Alice had some experience with employees at the antique shop where she worked, and they hadn't all been reliable. She didn't own Many Treasures— the shop belonged to Mrs. Kinjo and her son— but she had taken on enough of a management role that she knew a thing or two. If Alice had thought anything suspicious had happened to the previous employee of A Witch's Thrift Shop, she wouldn't have recommended Hazel for a job there.

"When I walked past A Witch's Thrift Shop today, I got the strangest feeling something bad was going to happen. I told Celeste, but she thinks it's just my anxiety," Liza said.

"Anxiety about Hazel? Do you not want her to work there? You could cancel the interview—"

"No." Liza shook her head. "Hazel's excited about it, and Celeste had to rearrange her schedule to do the interview after today's auction at the thrift shop."

"You'll get an earful if you cancel it." Alice chuckled.

Liza's gaze traveled to her children. Hazel was just putting in the order. Zade peered into the glass case, still searching for his meal. The smile on Liza's face looked like bittersweet nostalgia.

Alice thought long and hard before, her gut twisting as she resolved to ask Liza a question. After a pause, Alice said, "It's none of my business, and if you don't want to talk about it, I understand, but the kids told me their father hasn't contacted them since the divorce."

Liza shifted uncomfortably in her chair as she answered, "He moved to a nearby city."

"And you don't know where?" Alice asked.

"He has an office on the outskirts of Urbana, but I didn't tell the kids. I don't want them popping in on him."

Alice hadn't thought of that. Hazel might not be skilled in magic, but her brother had more than enough talent to travel to places magically within seconds. At least Alice thought so. She wasn't sure exactly how far a mage could travel using magic. Alice had only gone from one room to another with Naveed's help, and that much distance had made her nauseous.

"I should tell you that the kids have been trying to contact him themselves," Alice said.

Liza put a hand to her forehead, "They have been asking me about him more lately. I didn't realize they were trying to find him. That must be why they've been so secretive." Liza let out a soft laugh, adding, "I'm relieved. At least they're not investigating Mara's disappearance."

"Do you want to see Tom? I mean, for the kids?" Alice asked.

Liza hesitated, then reached for her purse rummaged through it. A few seconds later, she took out a crinkled, sealed envelope. "Months ago, I wrote Tom a letter asking him to see the kids, but I didn't have the courage to send it. I've been carrying it in my purse for weeks trying to work up the nerve."

"You've got the stamp on it and everything. If you need a little emotional support, I can be there for you when you put it in the mailbox," Alice said. Liza stared down at the letter, saying nothing. Alice tilted her head, gently asking, "Or I could send the letter for you?"

"Would you?" Liza quickly replied. "Oh, I'm sorry. I don't mean to put this on you, but it would be a help. I just don't think I'm brave enough to do it myself."

Alice reached out, and Liza handed her the envelope. "I'm happy to help," Alice said as she placed the letter in her purse.

For the first time this morning, the color seemed to return to Liza's pale face. Her relief was audible in her voice as she said, "You know, sometimes I think the best of all my talents is having a good sense of people. From the moment I saw you, I sensed a lot of goodness in you, Alice."

Liza and Alice both smiled as the kids walked up to the table.

"Two daily specials, a spinach croissant, and a pizza for the less sophisticated member of the group," Hazel said, setting the tray on the table.

Zade grabbed his pizza off the tray and took a bite before even sitting down. Oblivious to Hazel's eye-roll, he took his soda and gulped that down, too. Alice and Liza took their sandwiches and thanked Hazel.

"You make a good waitress, maybe you should work here," Alice remarked.

"No way. I'm going to be great at A Witch's Thrift Shop. I've got a knack for knowing about old objects and where they come from. I've even studied a bit about spelled objects and their histories."

Between bites, Zade said, "Yeah, she may not be Talented, but she sure knows magical antiques." This earned him a horrified look from his mother and an embarrassed, red-cheeked sulk from his sister. Zade wiped his mouth with his napkin and said, "Sorry."

Liza calmly explained to Alice, "We don't know for sure that she's Untalented, you know how some children are late bloomers."

Hazel said softly, "If I don't show any talent before I'm eighteen, I won't be allowed to visit Magic Row anymore. That's why I want this job: I want to be around magic items as long as I can."

"I understand." Alice felt her heart sinking. In part, she felt sorry for Hazel. Part of her also felt sorry for being here in Magic Row, pretending to be Talented while Hazel had to openly acknowledge that one day she might not be allowed to stay.

"Why don't we practice a little for your interview?" Liza successfully cheered her daughter with a change of subject.

"I know exactly how I'm going to impress Celeste," Hazel started.

While Hazel chatted about how excited she was for her interview and what she would say to Celeste's questions, Alice's attention wandered to the door. Sebastian Delvaux— level nine wizard, and owner of most of the buildings on Magic Row— made his entrance.

The tall, thin man with the bewitching blue eyes entered, spotted Titania Knight, and walked pointedly in her direction. Sebastian, or Baz, as he was known on Magic Row, shirked off his long, grey coat and tossed it up. Then he pointed a long, twisted wand in his right hand at the fabric, guiding it smoothly onto the chair beside Titania. Baz's business suit was finely pressed, not a wrinkle in sight. One might have thought by looking at him that this was a man who had it all figured out.

Baz wasn't broad-shouldered and buff like Ron, but he was handsome in a more refined manner. He wasn't charming, though, either. He had an irritating directness about him, a no-nonsense attitude that was off-putting on first meeting.

It had certainly put Alice off when he'd accused her of being Untalented and tried to hex her on the spot at their first meeting. Baz was right, of course, but Celeste had to convince him otherwise. Since then, he had saved Alice's life, so her opinion had changed. Alice wasn't sure if she should hate Baz for trying to hex her or love him for saving her life from a power-hungry witch. Not *love him*, love him. She was grateful. That was all.

Liza, noticing her gaze, leaned toward Alice, "Titania and Baz's engagement party is next Saturday. Every vendor on Magic Row is invited. I wouldn't be surprised if you received an invitation."

"I'm not sure I'd want to go," Alice said. There was a little too much honesty in Alice's tone. She blushed.

Liza didn't know about Alice's mixed feelings toward Baz, but she sensed something in Alice's response. "You're not happy for them?" Liza asked.

"It's not that," Alice said. "I don't really know them."

How well could one know a person they'd met twice? Their first meeting popped into her mind. Baz had grabbed her chin, tried to hex her to reveal she wasn't a witch. His eyes had been unreal, a deep, radiant blue, bursting with magic. She shuddered at the memory.

Zade, who had scarfed down his pizza, turned to his mother and asked, "Can we get dessert?"

Alice reached into her purse, but Liza put a hand out to stop her. "You got lunch, let me get dessert." Liza looked back at Zade, "Tell them to put in on my account."

"Awesome," Zade was in line in seconds.

Hazel wiped her lips with a napkin and rose, saying, "Alice, Mother, what can we get for you?"

Liza waved off dessert, with the excuse of an upset stomach. Alice, not one to refuse a kindness, said, "Surprise me."

Hazel left a half-eaten spinach croissant on her plate and joined Zade in line. Alice's attention went back to Baz and Titania. She couldn't help it. The pair seemed so incompatible. Baz didn't seem the type to go for shallow beauty; shallow and beauty were the two words most used by members of Magic Row to describe Titania. She couldn't have bewitched Baz, he was more powerful than her. But he was a man, after all, and Titania's combination of beauty and wealth must cast a spell few men could resist. Alice's average looks and empty pocketbook were almost a hex on her love life.

"We could go together and make a girl's night of it," Liza was saying.

It took Alice a moment to realize Liza was still talking about the engagement party. Alice needed to stop watching the couple. If she kept on looking, Liza would keep bringing up the subject, and Alice was sure she didn't want to go to an engagement party for a couple she barely knew. It would just be a reminder of how she was still single.

"No, thanks," Alice said. "You should go with a date, have fun. I could babysit if you want."

"The twins are fourteen. They'll be fine for a night. And I don't see myself going with anyone else."

"I don't know. I think I'd wait for Ron to ask," Alice teased.

Liza's smile dropped. "Oh. I didn't realize you and Ron…well, I…hope he does ask you."

"No," Alice said, "I didn't mean me, I meant I'd wait if I were you. Ron seems interested in you, Liza."

"Me?" Liza turned a subtle shade of pink.

Alice chuckled. "If this morning was anything to go by, I'd say he's definitely interested."

"He was just helping me with a case. And besides, everyone knows he's a flirt. He's like that with all the ladies," Liza rambled.

"He does flirt with all ladies," Alice said. It was part of why she had been skeptical about him hitting on Liza this morning, but once she thought about it, she reconsidered. He'd been a little flirty with Alice when they'd first met, but it was nothing like the way he looked at Liza. "He wasn't just flirting with you. He wasn't spouting lines or charming you with compliments — he was giving you his full attention like you were the only person in the room," Alice said.

"I…" Liza's argumentative tone transformed. "Do you really think so? I mean, he's younger than me…and I have two children...and," Liza paused. She looked at Hazel and Zade returning from the counter and said, "We really shouldn't talk about this in front of the children."

"I got you a strawberry scone." Hazel handed a white baggie to Alice. Hazel and Zade each had a giant brownie wrapped in plastic that would have been far more appetizing. But Alice said thank you and took the bag with a smile.

"Puck's outside," Zade said as he unwrapped his dessert.

Alice looked out the window but didn't see anyone. Instead, her eyes involuntarily returned to Baz and Titania, who rose from their table. Baz held a hand to help Titania up, she took it with a smile, but as she stood, she stole a glance at Alice's table. Alice tried to look away, but noticed in the last second that Titania wasn't looking at her. Titania's eyes traveled to Liza, and there was something in them that looked like fear. She was definitely worried about something. And Liza, who gave Titania a reassuring smile, seemed to know the trouble.

What had Liza told her in her reading? Or what secret had Titania told Liza that she now regretted divulging? Whatever it was, Liza was professional enough to keep it quiet. Alice reminded herself that it wasn't her business.

Her business was the orphan whom she could now see standing in the window of Reading and Co. holding a black cat. As soon as Titania and Baz walked out the door, Puck tapped on the window. He frowned through the glass.

"Why doesn't he come in?" Alice asked.

"He's banned," Liza said. "Almost every shop on Magic Row has accused him of shoplifting."

"That's terrible," Hazel said, pouting as she turned her eyes to Puck.

"Hard to believe. He's a pretty good thief. They never catch him," Zade said.

Puck had been caught just a few days ago by Naveed, but Alice didn't bring that up. Instead, she picked up her baggie with the strawberry scone and said, "Sorry, it looks like I have to leave a little early."

"Are you getting back the cat Puck stole?" Zade asked, looking out the window.

Hazel reprimanded Zade. "He didn't steal Fluffy. He was just borrowing him."

"How do you borrow a cat?" Liza asked.

"I'll see you guys after the auction," Alice said.

Outside, Puck set Naveed on the ground. Naveed let out a little growl and wandered over to Alice. Puck nodded and turned to walk away.

"Wait a minute," Alice said.

"Look, I didn't take your cat, he was with Hex—"

"I know—wait, he was where?" Alice raised an eyebrow at Naveed. Hex, the other genie on Magic Row, who also posed as a cat, had made it clear she did not want to talk to Naveed. She had avoided him at every turn, literally ducking down side streets whenever she saw him on Magic Row. Alice had told him to just leave her alone, but Naveed was determined to corner her into a conversation.

Naveed hung his head low and lay down on the pavement. Alice frowned. She wouldn't press him. "Puck, do want to take the cat with you on purpose this time?"

Naveed cocked his head and blinked at Alice. She kept her eyes on Puck, who had a very similar expression to the cat. Then he shook his head.

"I don't cat-sit," he said.

"It's not cat-sitting, but it is a job, if you want it," Alice said.

Puck crossed his arms. "What is it?"

Alice retrieved the letter and the business card from her purse. "It's nothing difficult, just take this letter to the address on this…" Alice paused. What had Belinda called it? "Open invitation card," Alice said.

"Why do I have to take the cat?"

"Can you turn yourself invisible?"

"I don't have an invisibility charm, only the people who work on Magic Row get that." Puck said.

"Well, then, that's why you need the cat," Alice said.

"Right, the invisible cat," Puck said. "What kind of a pet is he, anyway? Most of the witch's pets I know can only do simple tricks like understanding what a witch or wizard is saying."

"Well, Nav- I mean Fluffy is a special cat. Now, will you do it?"

"What do I get out of it?" Puck asked.

"A strawberry scone? Or anything else you want for lunch at Readings." Alice said.

Puck took her scone, asking, "This and a piece of apple pie from Witch's Brew Bakery?"

Alice smiled. "You got it. I'll pick it up right after the auction and meet you outside?"

"Deal." Puck took the card and letter. Looking at the card, he raised an eyebrow. "Magic Rowss, as in…"

"That's right, he's Hazel and Zade's father."

Puck looked through the window at Hazel and Zade. Alice was pretty sure his eyes lingered on Hazel, who was happily chatting with her mother, no doubt still on the topic of her interview. After a few seconds, Puck picked up Naveed in his arms.

The two disappeared, hopefully, to reunite a father with his family. Or to start a drama-filled disaster. Alice took another glance at the Willows. Sending the letter was the right thing, Alice reassured herself. Tom would contact Liza and the kids, and they would meet somewhere safe outside of Magic Row. Everything would work out as it should.

So, why was it just now occurring to Alice that Liza's premonition might not be about Mara, but about something much more personal? Alice wasn't sure, of course, but now she had the same feeling gnawing at the pit of her stomach. She swallowed, pushed it down, and ignored it. All she had done was help bring a family together.

What could possibly go wrong with that?

FIVE

Threats in the Thrift Shop

C rowds were always good for business. The police auction for magical items confiscated by the Urbana Police Department had been scheduled for noon that day. Already at 11:45am, quite a gathering had turned out at A Witch's Thrift Shop.

Belinda Witcher was standing in the front, taking pictures of Sebastian Delvaux as he shook hands with Celeste Bellamy, Ron Knight, and several other men and women in Urbana PD uniforms. Titania stood in the background, being beautiful and aloof. She occasionally remembered to smile.

There was something in Titania's look that most spectators would miss. On the surface, she was calm. But to anyone carefully observing, Titania seemed nervous. She adjusted her hair several times, pulled at the sleeves of her fitted sweater dress, and frowned often. Whenever she thought no one was looking, she stared at the back table of police auction items.

Titania tried to conceal her interest in the auction

items with smiles and poses for the camera. Occasionally, she'd glance at the table again, making her appear shifty-eyed and scheming. Titania seemed all-too-aware of Belinda's old-fashioned camera until it focused on someone else. In sync with the flash, Titania made a quick movement, a small flick of her index finger, aimed with precision at the auction table.

She didn't actually touch the table, but something had disappeared from the array of items, Alice was sure of it. She couldn't tell what was missing. Whatever it was wasn't something grand or noticeable.

Everything was on the inventory list, which begged the question: Why would Titania take something? She had to know she would be caught. The Knights had more than enough money for Titania to just buy whatever it was she had wanted, so it made no sense for her to steal.

"You could make it less obvious," Vestra, another employee of A Witch's Thrift Shop, with curves and a flirty personality, said. She came from behind and stood next to Alice.

"What?" Alice asked.

Vestra put her hands on her hips. "You are staring at Titania like you want to club her. You're jealous."

"What?" Alice had to laugh. It was so ridiculous. Except Alice's defensiveness made it appear true. Even she didn't know why she had such a strong reaction.

"I admit, I didn't really picture you with Baz, but I can see it now, and it might be worth a shot," Vestra said.

"I do not," Alice started off way too loudly. A few

customers turned their heads in Alice's direction. She brought it down a notch. "I do not want a shot a Baz." Alice looked around and whispered, "I thought I saw Titania pocket an item from the auction table."

Vestra looked puzzled and then looked over to the items on display. Baz was giving some sort of speech about how honored Magic Row was to be working with the Urbana PD— mage division. Celeste was looking nervous about public speaking. And Titania was making a getaway out of the store.

"Are you kidding? You can't make an accusation like that against a Knight, especially not in public like this. Besides, maybe you didn't see what you thought you saw," Vestra whispered.

It was a good point. Titania's brother, Ron, was a police officer, her fiance was Baz, and who knows who else she had in her corner? Alice couldn't accuse her. As to not seeing things right, if Alice hadn't known she was among witches, she would believe Vestra. Alice probably wouldn't have thought Titania had done anything at all. Titania hadn't physically gone near the table, after all, so to say she'd stolen something should be impossible. But Alice knew all the things a witch could do, and the impossible made the list nine times out of ten.

Alice walked toward the table, just to get a better view. And it was a good thing Vestra followed. Had the two of them continued standing so close to the window, they would have been hit with shattered glass.

Everyone ducked, Alice lower than anyone else— diving to the ground with her hands over her head. Before she had the courage to stand, Ron made his way to the door. Another officer, a brown-haired, muscular man in a uniform that read Q. Ramsey, had been positioned by the window. He turned to look outside.

"Did you see anything?" Ron asked.

"Someone outside threw something, sir. I didn't see who," Officer Ramsey said. He took a handkerchief from the pocket of his uniform, flicked it open, then bent to retrieve the object that had flown through the window. He held up a gray stone for Ron to see. Alice could make out a note wrapped around it.

"What does it say?" Celeste asked.

"Everyone, stay calm," Ron said, using the tip of Ramsey's handkerchief to pry the note away from the stone. It had either been glued or was otherwise stuck to the stone.

Alice could hear Baz say to Ron, "Now are you convinced?"

"What does the note say?" Celeste stormed over, her hands on her hips and a look more ferocious than fearful.

A bystander, who had a view of the note, burst out: "It says: 'Freaks.'"

"A message against mages?" Ramsey asked.

Baz raised his head, his eyebrow lifted as he looked at Ron. Ron was an inch or so taller than Baz, but somehow Baz managed to lord over him like he did everyone else in the magic community. At least that was Alice's impression. Baz looked directly at a person when speaking to them but in an *I'm-reading-your-thoughts* sort of way. It unnerved Alice, and judging by Ramsey's shifting eyes— even though he wasn't the target of Baz's gaze— it was having the same effect on him.

Another bystander, an old woman, interrupted Baz's stare with a panicked outcry, "Does that mean there is an Untalented in Magic Row?"

Alice's heart could have stopped. The whispers that broke over the previously pin-drop silent crowd translated into Alice's brain as *"It must be that new girl!," "I'll tell you who the Untalented is: We're staring right at her,"* and the direct accusation of *"It's Alice Adelcraft!"* Only Celeste's hand on her shoulder snapped Alice out of it.

Alice only caught the last two words Celeste said to her. "All right?"

Alice nodded. The whispers returned to what they were: untranslatable murmurs.

Through the side of her mouth, Celeste whispered, "You don't have to smile, but stop looking like you're guilty of something."

Alice let her breath go and tried for a relaxed expression. Her eyes scanned the room to see if anyone had noticed her tension. Everyone seemed too wrapped up in their own fears. Baz, however, looked Alice straight in the eye. This time she worried he really could read her mind.

"Let's not jump to any conclusions," Ron said to Ramsey. "Do an M-trace on the note and the stone, then take them down to forensics for prints." Ron addressed the rest of the crowd with, "Sorry, ladies and gentlemen, it looks like we're all going to be here for a while."

Over the moans and groans of protestation, a young male voice asked, "What if we didn't see anything?"

Alice was surprised to see Zade standing by the *Wands— On Sale This Week!* Sign. Hazel and Liza were there too, which was a blatant indication that Alice had been far too caught up watching Titania to be aware of her surroundings. Alice hadn't noticed them entering the shop. She hadn't seen the rock-thrower either.

"We still need a statement, but then you're free to go. Celeste, we should start with you?" Ron said.

Celeste and Alice exchanged a nod. Alice would be all right, especially now that Baz's ice-blue eyes weren't giving her the chills anymore. Baz, somehow exempt from all the rules, had gone outside.

Alice walked over to the Willows. "Are you all right?" Alice asked.

"Yes, we are." Liza put her arms on her son's and daughter's shoulders.

Hazel asked, "Do you think this has something to do with Mara's disappearance?"

"I don't know. But if it does, I'm sure we'll find out." Alice said, her ears already picking up on snippets of conversations.

Alice couldn't be sure, but she thought she heard, "woman," "slender," and "disappeared in a second," all of which described Titania to a T, including the magical ability. Alice was sure it was no Untalented throwing stones at mages. It was Titania.

She might have said something to Liza, Celeste, or one of the officers, but Ron approached the Willows.

Alice couldn't make any accusations against Titania to her brother, and he already looked upset.

"Liza, are you and the kids all right?" Ron asked, wrapping his hand on her shoulder in a firm grip.

Liza turned blush-pink. "We're fine," she said.

Ron smiled and let go, saying, "I'm glad. We won't hold you here long…" he trailed into a rambling conversation. The teens glanced at each other and at Alice. all three of them noticing that Ron's attention was squarely set on their mother. Twenty seconds in, Zade was over it and started wandering around the store.

Hazel followed, whispering, "Don't touch anything. I'm going to be working here soon…"

Alice walked the other direction herself, toward the front of the store, where she found Officer Ramsey kneeling by the broken glass. He held the stone in one gloved hand. His other hand hovered over it. Ramsey's eyes were closed but opened when Alice's shoe crunched on the glass.

"Sorry," Alice said, stepping back.

Ramsey studied Alice as if deciding whether or not to be angry or suspicious of Alice breaking her concentration. What actually came out of Ramsey's mouth was, "You're Alice Adelcraft?"

"Yes." Alice couldn't keep the surprise out of her voice. She waited for Ramsey to say more, but the officer just stayed at he was, watching Alice. Awkwardly, Alice said, "I, uh, didn't mean to break your concentration. I was just wondering what Ron, um, Officer Knight, meant by an M-trace?"

"A magic trace. If any magic has been used on this

object, I can find it and identify it." Ramsey was confident.

"Ah, you're tracing the magic to see if it was a mage or a regular person," Alice said.

Ramsey raised an eyebrow. "Regular person?"

Alarm widened Alice's eyes. "Untalented. I'm— I imagine that's how they'd think of themselves if they knew we were real." Alice swallowed hard. She had to back out of the conversation before Ramsey suspected her of being Untalented, or a "regular person" as Alice did think of it. "I'd better let you get to back to the M-trace before the magic wears off."

Ramsey said, "Yeah, that's a common misconception. Depending on the level of talent, a trained mage can detect spells on objects for years afterward— forever if the magic is strong enough."

"Even if other spells are used?" Alice asked.

"It's like fingerprints. There can be multiple sets, but we can usually figure out how many spells were used on an object and which ones were most recent."

Alice nodded. "And from there you can figure out who cast the spells. I've got it now, I just didn't realize it was called an M-trace."

Ramsey shook his head. "I'm no Baz. I don't have that kind of talent, and if I did, I'd certainly stay and offer my services." He grumbled under his breath. Ramsey had dark hair, broad shoulders, and a body that might have been muscular recently, though he had a layer of fat building and a subtle tinge of redness in his face. His brown eyes were neither piercing nor dull when he looked up at Alice. "Wait, can you tell who cast the spells?" Ramsey held the stone up to Alice as if willing to let her try.

"No." Alice held both hands up quickly enough that it might look like she was hiding something.

Ramsey shrugged and went back to performing the M-trace on the stone. "A lot of people think you're a ninth or even tenth level witch."

Alice could see Ramsey's observation for what it was: A police officer was fishing for information about Alice's level of talent. This was precisely what Alice needed to avoid. She had to deflect and do it in a way that didn't provoke suspicion.

Alice joked, "The rumors of my magic are greatly exaggerated."

Ramsey either didn't have much of a sense of humor or didn't care for Alice's wit. Or he didn't believe Alice. Worried he was onto her Untalented status, Alice added, "What if the rock isn't magic? What will you do then?"

Ramsey looked up at Alice as if he was talking to an imbecile. "There would still be fingerprints," Ramsey said.

"Right." Alice chuckled, the heat rising in her cheeks.

Ramsey returned to work. The air under his right palm began to move. Like a heatwave rising in the desert, the air distorted around the stone.

An instant later, the glass at Alice's feet shook. She jumped back, expecting a similar reaction from others, but no one else braced for an earthquake. Alice said a silent thanks that Ramsey's eyes had been closed. He might have wondered if Alice was a witch at all.

The broken shards of glass hit each other like wind chimes. Then the pieces came together in a series of clinks. The damage on the window reversed. A Witch's Thrift Shop was restored to its original state, and the rock in Ramsey's hand now held the note wrapped around the stone, just as it must have been before it had been thrown.

Alice breathed relief that the shaking glass bit was over. Everyone else seemed to be holding in their breath, looking at Ramey. Even Baz reappeared through the front door. Ramsey's eyes remained closed, his palm still hovering over the note.

Ron walked past Alice, inquiring, "What are the findings?"

Ramsey opened his eyes and stood. "There was no magic used on the stone," he said.

A gasp escaped the lips of some patrons of the shop. Several uttered the word "Untalented." Alice hadn't imagined it this time, but it wasn't directed at her. It was a general fear that their hidden street had been infiltrated with outsiders.

Celeste said, "That doesn't mean it was an Untalented who threw the stone. Any mage can throw a rock without magic." Alice hoped the crowd missed the glance Celeste made in Alice's direction. It was an unconscious flicker of the eye, but Celeste had to be thinking that if one Untalented had snuck into Magic Row, others might be following suit. She might even be thinking about turning Alice in to the police. Alice couldn't blame her.

But Baz said, "Celeste's point is valid. But it works both ways. If magic was used, it does not have to be a mage who used it."

"What do you mean?" Ron asked.

"Residual magic. I found an exact entry point on the street."

"What does that mean?" Zade asked.

Baz said, "Most likely, it means a witch or wizard has spelled an object to allow an Untalented entrance onto magic street."

SIX

An Untalented Entrance

A Witch's Thrift Shop emptied, except for a few customers who were still straggling toward the door. As they walked, they speculated about Untalented Urbananites they knew who might be guilty of this vandalism. Baz and Ron were speaking with Celeste about their own theories, Ramsey shooed everyone out the door. It did not stop some people— Alice included— from eavesdropping.

Baz was not pleased. He didn't try to hide the annoyance in his voice when Ron invited Liza to confer with them. "Why exactly is she here?"

Ron answered, "She reported a missing person who worked in the shop: Mara Blest. I thought that might be relevant to the case."

Baz turned to Celeste, "Why wasn't I informed of Miss Blest's disappearance?"

Celeste's mouth dropped, and she looked between Liza and Baz. "I didn't think she was missing. I thought she'd up and quit with no notice. It's not like that hasn't happened before."

"With Mara?" Ron asked.

Celeste shrugged. "Well, yes. A few years ago, she disappeared for a week. It turned out she had gone to some music festival. I almost fired her for that."

"Why didn't you?" Ron asked.

"She's mostly reliable. When Mara came back, she said it was a misunderstanding and that she thought she'd taken the time off," Celeste said.

Vestra, who made no attempt to hide that she had been eavesdropping, walked forward and spoke up quickly. "Is she really missing?"

"We're looking into every possibility. Did you notice anything strange in the last few days? Was she frightened, or did she mention anyone scaring her?" Ron said.

"No, why?" Celeste asked.

"Do you think someone hurt her? Was she kidnapped?" Vestra asked.

"We're investigating every possibility," Ron said.

"I live in her building," Vestra said.

"Did you see anything, hear anything?"

"No, I'm not on the same floor. If someone is targeting witches… am I next?" Vestra clutched her heart and looked at Ron in terror.

Ron held a hand up reassuringly. "There's no reason to believe that," Ron said.

"Do you think her disappearance is related to the rock-throwing?" Celeste asked.

"Anything is possible, but I don't see how they're

related. This seems a lot more like an Untalented who has somehow entered Magic Row," Ron said.

"They would need help. Residual magic suggests someone Talented bewitched an object allowing them entrance."

"Who would let an Untalented into Magic Row?" Ron asked.

Alice could not listen anymore. She had her own theory of who had thrown the rock, and it made her feel sick. Alice left the main area, following the clicking sounds of Belinda's camera.

Alice found Belinda taking pictures of the shop window, and tapped her on the shoulder. Belinda turned slowly, either not noticing or not caring about the distressed look on Alice's face. Belinda snapped one more picture before looking away from the lens.

"I need to speak to you. ASAP," Alice said.

Belinda nodded. She followed Alice past the front window toward the register. The space was currently empty of any audience. Alice glanced around, just to make sure they were alone.

When she was sure it was safe, Alice whispered, "Tom wouldn't have thrown that note, would he?"

Belinda blinked, surprised, "What? How could you think that?"

Alice felt the tightness in her chest, relaxing. What was she thinking? It couldn't have been Tom. Tom was a respected lawyer, or he was a lawyer, at any rate. Alice had no idea about his reputation. But she doubted he'd have come to Magic Row just to throw a rock in the window of a shop where his ex-wife and children were standing. Some Untalented person had thrown the rock, though, and now the whole mage community would be looking for the intruder. No Untalented person was safe.

"Tom shouldn't come to Magic Row now," Alice said.

"I agree. But there's no reason he would come here this morning. I haven't spoken to him today," Belinda said.

Alice winced. Belinda lowered her camera and put a hand on her hip. "You haven't spoken to him today, have you?" Belinda asked.

Alice didn't want to say that she had sent him a letter. She didn't know Belinda, but she definitely didn't want to make a big deal out of what was likely nothing. And she did not want to be involved in another investigation on Magic Row.

Naveed appeared in cat form behind Belinda. He moved forward, claws out, and shoulders back as if on the prowl. Did he think Belinda's camera pointing at Alice was a weapon? Alice moved around Belinda and picked Naveed up.

"Never mind. Everything is fine," Alice said, walking away with Naveed. Then she turned back. She may not have wanted to get involved in an official investigation, but that didn't stop her from doing a little digging of her own.

"Belinda, did you take pictures of everything on the auction table?" Alice asked.

"From every angle. Why?" Belinda said.

"Could I see them?" Alice asked.

"Not right now, sorry. I've got to run, or I'll be late

for my next appointment." Belinda reached into her bag and pulled out that handy card-carrier, sliding another card out. "You can call me anytime."

Belinda handed the card to Alice, who admired the transparent design. It looked the way a camera lens did when one was looking into it to take a picture. The snapshot it focused on was Belinda's name, phone number, and address.

"You live in Urbana Gardens?" Alice noticed.

"I know. It's strange having a studio in an apartment. And it's not mage territory. But I can't really afford rent in any—"

"No, no, I don't mean that. I live in Urbana Gardens. If you could just take a few pictures of the table again and we could meet there— I just need to compare something."

"There's something different about the inventory before and after? Did someone take something?" Belinda asked, readying her camera for an intriguing shot.

"I'd rather not say until I'm sure." Alice would be careful not to accuse Titania. She had a feeling both Ron and Baz would not hear an allegation like that without proof. Alice didn't want to get thrown out of Magic Row for a faux pas like that any more than she wanted to get hexed for being Untalented.

Belinda, fortunately, didn't need much convincing to take her snapshots. She was already adjusting her lens as she asked, "Come by tonight at 7pm if that works."

"Seven works fine. Thanks," Alice replied.

As Belinda walked away, Alice turned her attention

to the cat in her arms. Naveed's black eyes were trained on Belinda until she disappeared around the shelves. He kept staring when she was out of sight.

"Naveed." Alice had to whisper his name twice before Naveed looked at her. Something was distracting him, but Alice would have to deal with that later. She bent down and set him on the ground.

"Where is Puck?" Alice asked.

Naveed looked up at her with more apathy than usual—which was hard to beat for the cat-jinn. Then he blinked and looked back out the window.

"What is wrong with you?" Alice asked, genuinely concerned this time.

Naveed meowed. Alice spotted Puck in the window, surrounded by Hazel and Zade, who were speaking excitedly. Alice imagined they were telling him all about the attack on the thrift shop. At least Puck was safe and well.

Alice bent down and petted Naveed's ear. She was surprised he let her do it. Softly, Alice said, "I know something's bothering you, and I promise we'll talk about it later. Right now, I need you to go to Tom Willows' office and take back a card from him. It's a business card that looks just like the one I gave you and Puck earlier."

Naveed nodded. He looked out the window. Alice knew what he was asking, and she responded, "No. Don't take Puck. He doesn't need another theft on his record. And you can probably find it better on your own."

Naveed disappeared without so much as a growl.

That was not like him. Alice made up her mind to confront Naveed about his sulking later, but for now, she was glad he disappeared without anyone noticing.

At least she thought he had. As Alice lifted her eyes to the window, Baz stopped in the middle of the road. He and Ron must have just left. They were clearly parting ways when Baz turned around and looked directly at Alice. In her periphery, Alice could see the twins chatting with Puck, Belinda walking out of the store, and Ramsey removing the floating yellow police tape. But Baz's focus was so intense, Alice wondered if all he could see was that she, Alice Adelcraft, was not a witch.

Alice's eyes widened. She blushed, turned around abruptly, and walked back behind the shelves. Once Alice was sure she was out of sight, she put her back against the broomsticks and breathed in. He probably wasn't even looking at me. He was looking back at the store, that's all, Alice told herself.

"Hey, are you O.K.?" Vestra asked.

"Yes," Alice said before she realized Vestra wasn't talking to her.

Liza was staring out the window with her mouth open and her eyes wide. She looked like she'd seen a ghost. When she spoke, it was a barely audible whisper that sounded like, "I don't believe it."

"What's going on?" Celeste asked.

Ignoring the question, Liza took a step toward the door.

"Hello, Liza," a male voice came from the doorway. Alice and Vestra walked past the shelves in time to see a thin man with sandy brown hair in a brown coat and leather shoes. He smiled faintly, but there was a certain sorrow in his brown eyes conveying loss or guilt, likely both.

"Tom?" Liza asked.

"I don't believe it," Celeste said.

"Tom? Isn't that…" Vestra began, but Celeste elbowed her in the side.

"May I come in?" Tom held a hat in his hands, which he used to gesture to the inside of the store.

He was asking Liza, but Celeste, whose shop it was, answered, "I think you'd better come inside, and explain how an Untalented entered Magic Row."

SEVEN

Unexpected Arrivals

"I saw your letter, and it made me want to...well, I have this card, and, I can't explain it...but I concentrated on...on you, Liza, and it brought me here," Tom said.

Despite his flummoxed speech, Tom's voice was smooth and deep. The navy blue business suit was predictable lawyer attire, but the fit suggested a surprisingly tone man of tall stature. With his hazel eyes and masculine features, he was a definite competition for Ron Celeste stepped forward. "What card? Where did you get it?" Celeste asked with her hands on her hips.

"A friend." Tom said. He looked down his nose at Celeste, adding, "If you don't mind, I'd rather speak with Liza alone."

Liza did not seem to be over her shock. She didn't say anything. Tom said her name a few times, but only stirred Liza enough to make her look out the window at Hazel and Zade. Alice was thankful they were still distracted by their conversation with Puck. They hadn't seen their father, and, considering none of them knew

Tom's true intentions in coming here, that might be a good thing.

Vestra stepped forward, volunteering. "I'll take the kids for some lunch."

"They've had it," Liza said absently, turning her eyes back to her estranged ex-husband.

Alice spoke up. "Kids never mind a second dessert. If it's OK with Liza, you could take them to A Witches Brew Bakery."

Vestra looked at Liza, who nodded.

"Could you take Puck with you? I'll pay you back."

Vestra's lips dipped down. She wasn't a fan of Puck, Alice knew, but she was still a good sport. Vestra said with fake cheer, "Sure. I'd be happy to." Then, she smiled at Tom as she went past him toward the door.

Celeste walked between Liza and Tom, saying, "All right, you can use my office."

"I'd prefer mine," Tom said. He lifted the card in his hand. "I'm not sure how all this works, but I think I can get back using this." He reached a hand out to Liza. "I'm not sure I'm worthy of asking, but will you hear me out?"

Liza's eyes fluttered. She gave a tight smile, the kind that acted as a dam, holding back a rush of tears. Nodding, Liza took Tom's outstretched hand, then she gasped.

"What about Hazel's interview?" Liza turned to ask Celeste. It was interesting to see that even in complete shock, Liza was still thinking first like a parent.

Celeste said, "I'll do it in a little while. Let them have a little fun first."

"I can go get her when Celeste is ready," Alice said.

Liza smiled in appreciation and looked back at Tom. Tom smiled back at her and flipped the card between his fingers. The two of them disappeared.

"Well, that was strange," Celeste said.

"Yeah," Alice said, putting a hand to the back of her neck. She didn't look Celeste directly in the eye for fear of letting anything slip. Celeste saw through her in a second.

"Alice, do you know anything about the rock?" Celeste asked.

"No. Why would you ask me that?" Alice said.

Celeste crossed her arms. "Then you know how or why Tom showed up just now."

"No. Maybe. Look, I just wanted to help." Alice held her hands up, giving up defending herself.

"Tell me everything," Celeste said.

She waved a hand, flipping the sign on the shop door to closed using her magic. Then she beckoned Alice to follow her to the office in the back. Alice explained about Tom and Belinda's card, and the twins' plan to get their father back.

"Poor kids," Celeste said. "It was terrible when Tom left."

"The kids said it was because he found out about magic."

"That would be all the kids knew."

"You mean there's more?"

"Not really. Liza never said anything, but I always got the feeling she thought he was too interested in other women."

"She thought he was cheating?"

"From her perspective, all he did was flirt. Liza kept asking us questions like if it was normal to have so many women's phone numbers in his phone or to have a woman join Tom for lunches all the time. I remember Liza saying Tom seemed very close with his secretary, too."

"That doesn't necessarily mean he was cheating," Alice said.

"Now you sound like Liza. She was always justifying the late nights at the office if you know what I mean. It sure painted a picture that was obvious to the rest of us."

"So you think finding out about magic wasn't the only reason he left?"

"From what Liza said, he freaked out about that for sure. But, he did seem like he wanted out of the marriage a long time before that. That happens sometimes when people marry young."

"How did Tom find out about magic?"

"There's the rub. They needed money while Tom was finishing law school, and Liza started using her talent to read futures. Tom was fine when he thought it was all nothing. Then he started to see more and more that it was real. And when Zade started showing magical abilities…well, Liza couldn't leave him in the dark anymore."

"She told him."

"Mmhmm. And it was all downhill from there." Celeste said.

"Liza told you all this, but you never met Tom before? You didn't seem to recognize him."

"Tom has never been to Magic Row until this morning."

"He didn't throw the rock," Alice said quickly.

Celeste raised an eyebrow. "Then you know who did?" she asked.

"No. I just…don't think it was Tom," Alice said. "There was a similar incident at the museum. The paintings in the Witchy Ways exhibit were all ruined,"

"A witch exhibit? You think whoever did this also vandalized the museum paintings?" Celeste looked thoughtful.

"It was the same word, Freaks painted in red on the portraits," Alice said.

"Did you tell Ron?" Celeste asked.

Alice frowned. "I didn't think about it. Maybe Belinda did."

"I think you should, especially since Mara's disappearance might be a kidnapping."

"I don't see how the vandalism could be related to Mara's disappearance."

"The mage community is a small one. You'll often find that everything magical in Urbana is related in one way or another, so I won't be surprised if there's a connection."

"Then I'll just have to find out what that connection is," Alice said as if to herself.

"Why exactly is it you who has to figure this all out yourself? Alice, you're not even one of us—oh, that didn't come out right. What I mean is you're risking your neck every time you come to Magic Row, just by secretly being a you-know-what."

"Untalented?" Alice said.

"Don't admit that aloud, not even when you think you're alone. And yes. Alice, you need to keep a low profile around here. You seem determined to go to extra lengths to get yourself discovered. You don't realize how dangerous witches and wizards can be—especially when they feel their safe spaces are being invaded." Celeste got up. The coffee machine sputtered out the last drop, and Celeste picked up two coffee cups and brought them and the freshly brewed pot over to the table.

"You found out, and you haven't threatened to turn me into a brain-dead zombie," Alice said.

"That's not an accurate description of the curse they'll put on you. Or maybe it's fair—memory hexes are tricky. Anyway, I'm open-minded. If Baz or Rhys find out who you are…"

"It's too late for that," Alice said.

Celeste nearly dropped the whole pot of coffee mid-pour. Luckily, with her magic, Celeste was able to freeze the entire coffee pouring situation. She let go of the coffee pot, cup, and saucer and put a hand to her chin. Alice just stared at the suspended brown liquid waterfall, or coffee-fall, rather. Celeste paced a few times around the table.

Finally, she asked, "Baz or Rhys? Which of them knows?"

"Rhys."

"By the moon!" Celeste scratched her forehead, "OK, OK, he hasn't hexed you yet, so it can't be that bad."

"Celeste, calm down."

"Why are you calm?" Celeste asked, "I could maybe get in a little trouble for knowing about you, but you… you could get your memory wiped clean!"

"He knows that I'm an Adelcraft. He knew my family."

Celeste quirked her head and sat down. Slowly, she said, "So, you really are that kind of Adelcraft, or does he just think you're related to that mage family?"

"He believes it, but I think it may also be true. He said he knew an Adelcraft who married an Untalented, and he knew my father had died of natural causes and that my mother had died in a fire. He thought I had died, too."

"Why would he think you were dead?"

"I don't know. I haven't worked up the courage to ask him more about it. It's…I thought I'd buried those feelings…" Alice couldn't go on. She had been eight years old when the fire happened, but she couldn't remember much of it. She had blocked it out and, she suspected, for good reason.

"It must have been traumatic for you." Celeste reached over and patted Alice's hand.

Alice smiled faintly. "I was thinking if my father was a wizard, maybe I'm not pretending to fit in here. Maybe I am a witch, too."

"Oh, honey. It doesn't always work that way."

"But Zade has magic," Alice said.

"It's like blue eyes or blond hair; if both parents don't have it somewhere in their genes, the kids don't inherit the trait. Tom's family must have had some magic somewhere in the past. That's how it works."

"Magic is a recessive trait?" Alice said. "But we don't know for sure my mother didn't have the gene."

"No," Celeste said, "But it's rare. There are no more than fifty thousand Talented people the world over. Actually, fifty is pushing it. I'm sorry to say, it's just not common enough to assume someone has it."

Alice felt like a two-year-old, pouting because she just found out magic wasn't real—not for her, anyway. But she couldn't help it. She had a little hope that she was special, after a lot of disappointing moments in life which had shown her she was not. Celeste resumed the coffee pouring and handed Alice a cup.

"Looks like you need this, hon. I really am sorry."

"It's fine," Alice said. She took the cup, looking up to see Celeste's sympathetic frown. Pity was not a good look. Alice didn't like seeing it directed at her. She reiterated, "I'm fine. Really. It's not like I've ever been able to do magic anyway. I should have known by now that I don't have, you know, talent."

Celeste poured her own cup, saying, "People know by the time their seventeen. I don't know why that's the magic number if you'll forgive the pun. But if you don't show ability by then, it's pretty much understood that you won't show talent for your whole lifetime."

"Then I guess I'm out." Alice pushed back her coffee cup and stood up. "I really appreciate the coffee, but I've got the afternoon shift at Many Treasures. I don't want to be late," Alice said.

"You want the coffee to go?" Celeste asked, waving a hand to open a cupboard. A Styrofoam cup floated out.

Alice put up a hand. "No, thanks. I don't really feel like drinking anything."

What Alice felt like drinking was stashed in a cabinet she rarely opened back in her apartment. She liked to save those for actual parties rather than the self-pitying kind. When she smiled at Celeste while saying good-bye, she tried thinking positively instead.

Alice had spent twenty-eight years without magic. She didn't need it now. But it hit her then that Alice hadn't been around witches and wizards her whole life, so now might be the very time she did need magic. Come to think of it, Alice realized that her father had died of a heart attack, and her mother had burned in a fire that had left Alice orphaned. Who's to say she hadn't needed magic then?

Magic might have made all the difference in Alice's life. It might have helped Alice save her mother. As she walked across the street to Many Treasures, Alice mused on how different life might have been if she was talented. She regretted that she didn't have the magical ability to stop that fire. It was the sort of thing that made her envious of the mages.

It was the sort of thing that might make an Untalented person jealous. Alice was a little jealous, and she had just recently found out about mages. Alice wondered what it must be like for a witch or wizard growing up Untalented in the mage community. Could someone like Hazel grow up to be jealous of her brother Zade?

Was the person who threw the rock angry that magic existed or envious that it was out of reach?

EIGHT

Nearly Caught

Most people disliked their workplaces. Alice loved Many Treasures antique shop. Never had she imagined A Witch's Thrift Shop was hidden directly across the street from the shop, but it just made it all the more special to Alice. *'Special'* could be overwhelming sometimes, though, like it was now.

The weight of Magic Row's problems pressed on Alice's mind, but she felt lighter with every step closer to the Many Treasures. Magic Row faded entirely as Alice reached a large, grey dumpster. The scene around Alice became an alleyway the moment her foot touched the sidewalk pavement.

Except, unlike every other regular day, today the alleyway was crowded. Witches and Wizards, some in normal attire and some in their mage robes, stood around conversing. A few wandered into Many Treasures' side door, the one they used for nothing more than taking out the trash.

"Oh, excuse me," an older woman said as she

bumped into Alice. She might have been taller than Alice— almost everyone was— except that age had warped her posture so that she bent forward and leaned on her cane to walk.

"Do you need help?" Alice asked. She reached for the door, opening it for the woman.

The woman had a kindly face with round glasses and just enough wrinkles to soften her eyes as she smiled and said, "Thank you. I like this new shop, but they made it hard to enter, hiding the door beside a dumpster. All this garbage sends a bad message to customers."

Alice considered explaining to the old woman and the other mages that this was the alley and that customers had to go around the side to enter the front of the shop. Several of the witches and wizards had figured that out, but apparently not all—not even half. Did they not see an alleyway like Alice saw? When they turned around, was the view still Magic Row for them? If it was, Alice realized, her explanation would only cause more confusion.

Alice smiled, saying, "I'll let the owners know."

She wasn't sure what she'd tell Mrs. Kinjo or her son Eric. The Kinjos, the owners of the shop, were Untalented and couldn't understand this sudden influx of new, strange customers. Alice hadn't told them about how she'd discovered Magic Row. She couldn't explain how the witches and wizards had assumed that Many Treasures was run by one of the Talented. Now that the shop was considered part of their community, these mages were labeling the antique shop a "new" edition to their shopping route.

It wasn't bad for business. The witches and wizards adored the antiques they sold. Some of the items, it turned out, were magical or at least had magical applications, which had thrilled Alice and confused Eric to no end.

Alice wasn't sure if Mrs. Kinjo believed the customers' stories about the magic of the objects, but she joined in with myth, legends, and magical tales of her own that she'd heard from her anthropologist husband. The late Mr. Kinjo had been something of a treasure hunter and, based on the stories of him, seemed to be the kind who would believe in such things as magic—in myth if not in reality. Mrs. Kinjo spent more time downstairs now that she had people inter- ested in her late husband's adventures, which was good for her since she spent so much time alone.

It also allowed the Kinjos to blend in just enough that the witches and wizards assumed they belonged on Magic Row.

So far, the question of who was Talented and Untal- ented hadn't come up, and Alice was grateful for that. She was also nervous about how long that would last.

Eric, Mrs. Kinjo's grandson, was a student of astronomy and a man of reason. Eric was the definition of all-work and no-play. He was a couple years younger than Alice, but even at 26 was laser-focused on becoming an astronaut. But even Eric wouldn't say the magic was in the stars. For him, science held all the awe he could handle. Magic would mess with his mind.

If anyone was going to blow their cover, it was Eric — especially when Vestra came around. Alice couldn't blame Vestra for taking an interest in Eric. She never thought of Eric that way, but he was tall, fit, and handsome if one were judging his looks. All Alice knew was that he kept to his exercise-and-study regime going with annoying devotion. Eric insisted Alice give him plenty of notice when taking time off because it messed with his schedule.

Inconveniences aside, Eric's workouts had paid off enough to gain Vestra's attention. Vestra was in the shop now, leaning over the counter in just the right way for Eric to get a view down her blouse. Poor Eric was enchanted. Torn between the influx of customers and Vestra's corset waistline, Eric looked relieved when Alice walked in.

"Finally," he said, "You wouldn't believe how busy it's been."

What could Alice say? She couldn't explain that the customers of A Witch's Thrift Shop had come to Many Treasures instead after a rock-in-the-window scare.

"Sorry I'm late." Alice walked up to the counter.

"That's OK, I've been helping with the customers," Vestra said.

"Seems like everyone's upset. Did you hear anything about this vandalism in a thrift shop?" Eric asked.

Alice frowned. She hadn't told Vestra Eric was Untalented, just like she hadn't told Eric Vestra was a witch. She was hoping to entirely avoid that conversation, but that seemed unlikely now.

"That's because A Witch's Thrift Shop just closed," Vestra said.

"A Witch's Thrift Shop? What a name." Eric shook his head.

"I know," Vestra said. "I was all for calling it The Thrifty Witch, but Celeste wouldn't go for it."

Eric raised an eyebrow. "People really go to a thrift shop like that here? I guess I shouldn't be surprised. There's a lot of interest in stuff like that at Urbana college."

"Oh yeah, a lot of our customers are college students. They can't afford the brand new stuff," Vestra said.

They seemed to be on the same page, but they were in two different books. Only Eric was not one to miss little things. Eventually, he would realize the miscommunication if Vestra, Hazel, or Zade ever tried a deeper conversation.

Alice interrupted, "Hazel, you'd better get back. Celeste should be ready for your interview now."

"Oh my gosh, OK. Wish me luck!" She said.

Zade asked, "Is mom still at the thrift shop? Do you think she'd be OK with me hanging out here a while? Mrs. Kinjo just went upstairs to get her collection of ancient compasses."

Eric chuckled. "They're not exactly ancient. But she does have one she's convinced is a Viking sunstone, so I guess that counts."

"Cool! Puck, do you want to stay and see them?"

"Nah, you go ahead. I've got more important things to do," Puck said.

"Like what?" Zade asked.

Alice could see in his eyes that Zade was a little hurt. She saw it all the time in the orphanage, the older boys disregarding the younger ones' interests, and the younger boys wanting to do whatever the older boys were doing. It was a typical kid behavior, and not surprising that Puck's and Zade's age gap would cause the same problem.

Alice said, "Puck's got another errand to do for me. Otherwise, I'm sure he would have been interested, right?"

Puck's lips pulled to the side in a half scowl at Alice, but he said to Zade, "Yeah, that's right."

"Aw, sorry. I'll see if she can show you the interesting ones another time," Zade said. He spied Mrs. Kinjo coming down the stairs and made his way around the other customers to get to her.

"Do you really have another chore for me? Because if this is a regular thing, I'm going to need actual payment," Puck said.

"Fair enough. I'll give you ten dollars on completion of your task."

"And that is?" Puck asked.

"Find Fluffy. He's run off again."

Puck rolled his eyes but left in search of the cat. A few seconds after Puck walked out of the store, Alice caught sight of a person in a hooded sweatshirt outside. He was hanging around the front with his head down and something red in his hands.

"Vestra," Alice said, watching the hooded figure.

"Yeah?" Vestra's half-smile faded. "Who is that?" she asked.

"I don't know, but that sure looks like a spray paint can," Alice said.

The hooded man looked up. A painters' mask on his face made it difficult to identify him. All Alice could see was a few strands of brown hair sticking out of the hood.

"Is that Puck?" Vestra asked.

"I just sent Puck on an errand," Alice said. Besides that, Puck had red hair. Alice thought the vandal's hair was brown, but when she looked again, the hooded figure had turned his head, and the sun hit the strands in such a way as to show the red highlights.

"I don't believe it," Alice said.

There was no reason for Puck to want to target witches and wizards. He was clearly magical himself!

Alice had seen him literally disappear around building corners before, hadn't she? If it was Puck, perhaps Alice could reason with him. She'd have to catch him first.

The figure ditched the spray paint and ran. Alice dodged the same lady she'd helped earlier and ran out the door. "Sorry!" she called out.

The old woman exclaimed, "My goodness!" as Vestra also passed her to the door.

Vestra dashed outside and caught up with Alice in seconds. She had her wand out and pointed at the boy. Alice always thought witches needed to speak words to do magic, but Vestra didn't say a word.

A spark of light shot out of her wand, and the perpetrator was pulled back. He grunted as he skidded across the floor onto his back. The door to Many Treasures opened, and Eric stepped out.

"What's going on?" He asked.

"You caught the vandal!" A voice behind Alice said.

She, Eric, Vestra, turned around to see Puck standing by the corner of Many Treasures with his hands in his pockets. Naveed, at his feet, raised his tail and readied himself for Alice's order to attack. Everyone turned their eyes back to the culprit, who was still sprawled on the floor.

"If Puck is here, who is that?" Alice asked.

"Time to find out." Vestra raised her wand, pointing it to the mask on the culprit's face.

Just as the magic shot from her hand, the boy clutched an amber stone around his neck, and disappeared.

"Did he just...Did you..." Eric started. He put his hands to his forehead, staring at the now empty space on the pavement.

"Looks like he left a message," Puck said, pointing to the corner of the brick building.

Fresh red paint formed the letter "F" and dripped down the wall. Just below it, the spray paint can lay abandoned. Puck reached to pick it up.

"No, don't touch it. You don't want your fingerprints on the evidence," Alice said.

"Some evidence. The police won't get any fingerprints off it, the man was wearing gloves," Vestra said.

"Ron might still be able to get some information from it. Maybe they can find out where it was purchased or something." Alice walked over and bent down. She looked at Naveed.

On cue, he looked at the bag and blinked. It was now safely sealed in a plastic bag. Alice picked it up.

"We've got to turn this over to the station."

Puck put his hands up, "Don't look at me. You already thought I was the vandal." The annoyance in his voice stung.

Alice winced. "I'm sorry. I didn't really think…" she began.

Vestra interrupted. "Never mind. We know it wasn't you." She pointed her wand at the wall and the paint erased itself in front of their eyes.

"OK, that's not right." Eric began to pace, taking deep breaths and holding his head like he'd lose his mind if he let go. "You're erasing it with…nothing…and you shot a spark out of a…it's a wand…you have a wand…which means…" He stopped pacing.

"Eric?" Alice said.

Eric dropped his hands, straightened his shoulders, and looked Vestra directly in the eyes. He looked as if he'd just discovered the world had ended. In a way, the world as he knew it was gone.

Eric whispered in shock, "That was magic."

NINE

Magic at Many Treasures

Alice opened the door for everyone to go back inside. Naveed, still a cat, walked into Many Treasures with his head hung low. Alice almost asked him what was wrong, but if Naveed answered in cat form, Eric was liable to have a seizure. Eric was Alice's main concern now.

As everyone walked back inside Many Treasures, Eric seemed to lose his power of speech. His mouth opened and closed several times. Vestra looked at Alice with an eyebrow raised.

Alice put a hand on Eric's shoulder. "Are you all right?" she asked.

"What did she just do?" Eric pointed at Vestra.

Vestra looked thoroughly confused. "All I did was a levitation spell."

"*Spell?*" Eric asked.

Puck, who walked inside last, leaned beside the door with his arms crossed and asked, "He doesn't know about magic?"

Eric looked at Puck. It might have been the smirk Puck wore that did it. Or maybe the confusion on Vestra's face or Alice's wincing that was the final straw. Eric snapped back to reality.

"Everyone out, we're closing!" Eric yelled.

"What?" The old lady customer asked.

"He says they're closing," said a gentleman in a checkered suit.

"That's right, closing. Everyone, please leave. I'm locking up." Eric walked around the counter and picked up his set of keys. He shooed the customers with his hands.

"What's going on?" Zade asked.

Putting his hands back in his pockets, Puck shrugged. "I think he's lost it."

"He's Untalented, isn't he?" Vestra whispered to Alice.

Alice didn't answer. Several panicked thoughts swirled around her head, primarily that she should have prepared the Kinjo's for Magic Row. Or Alice should have stressed to the mages that Many Treasures was not a part of Magic Row. She had never claimed that it was, but she could have helped stop the misconception. What if the Kinjos' memories were hexed because of her?

Mrs. Kinjo walked to the front of the shop. Her cane clicked as she went. Zade offered her a hand when she reached the counter. With Zade's help, Mrs. Kinjo sat on the stool.

"Now, tell me what has my grandson so upset."

"Hamee," Alice said the Okinawan word for

"grandmother." She continued, "I'm glad you're sitting down. There's something I have to tell you."

"They're witches, Baa-baa," Eric said. Eric's mastery of Japanese was not as perfect as his mastery of physics, but his Okinawan was non-existent. His use of the Japanese children's term for grandmother always made the corner of Mrs. Kinjo's lip turn down, just a little. Eric never noticed, but Alice did. Mrs. Kinjo frowned like that as Eric locked the side door and pulled down the window shade.

"So?" Mrs. Kinjo asked her grandson.

"So? So, they have *magic*! Real, actual magic, and they just used it on our building!"

"Only to get the paint off." Vestra pointed at the window with her wand.

"Stop pointing that thing around this shop!" Eric said.

"This *thing* happens to be a family heirloom," Vestra said, coming dangerously close to pointing her wand at Eric.

Alice stepped between them and held a hand up. "OK, I think we all just need to calm down."

"Calm down! How long have you been a witch?" Eric pointed his finger at Alice now.

"Yeah, how long, Alice?" Puck grinned.

Alice squinted at Puck. *What was he grinning about? Did he somehow know she wasn't a witch?* Alice couldn't worry about that now. She focused on Eric.

"Look. I know this is a lot to take in, but I'm still me, and things are…mostly the same. It's just, some of our customers are going to be…witches…and wizards from here on out. But they don't mean you any harm," Alice said. She turned to Vestra, nodding with her head to hint that she should put away her wand.

Vestra did so, but not without attitude. "You could have told me he was Untalented," Vestra said. Her lips thinned in annoyance as she tucked her wand into her sleeve. It disappeared. Alice couldn't figure out how, but she was glad it was no longer pointing at Eric.

"Untalented? I have plenty of talent." Eric shook his head and looked at Alice, "You could have told me she was a witch."

"Why are you acting like this?" Mrs. Kinjo asked. Eric looked at her, blinking. Mrs. Kinjo kept a stern expression directed at her grandson. "I have told you about magic all your life. What do you think your grand-father searched for in all of his travels? Magical items."

"But those were just stories," Eric said.

"Stories, yes. Your grandfather's life stories. You decided they were not real, that doesn't make it so."

"Are you Talented? Or was your husband?" Zade asked.

"You mean: Did we have magic?" Mrs. Kinjo asked. Zade nodded. "No, child. But I have seen it," Mrs. Kinjo said.

"And then you told everyone about it?" Vestra asked. She looked worried.

That was exactly what the mages worried about. They didn't want stories of witches and wizards circu-lating the globe. They wanted to remain hidden, and they'd hex any Untalented who might expose their secret.

"No, I never told my stories to anyone who would believe it. Except for Alice." Mrs. Kinjo smiled kindly in Alice's direction.

"This can't be real," Eric said.

"Oh, it's real," Puck said, still smirking like he was enjoying this immensely.

"Puck, maybe you and Zade should go," Alice said.

"Just when it gets interesting," Zade whined.

"Wait, what are they going to tell people?" Vestra asked.

"You can't tell them they're Untalented," Alice said, her eyes were wide and pleading as she looked at Puck and Zade.

"What do you mean 'Untalented?'" Eric asked.

"You don't have magic," Vestra said. She said it almost the same way Eric had accused her of being a witch. There was a moment of silence. Zade looked between Eric and Vestra and backed toward the door.

"What happens if they tell?" Eric asked quietly.

"They'll hex your memory," Alice said.

"Maybe I don't want to remember this," Eric said, glancing at Vestra. Vestra's eyes began to tear. She shook her head and took out her wand.

"No, Vestra, don't." Alice held a hand up toward Vestra, then looked at Eric and said, "Memory spells aren't stable. Memories are linked, it's not always possible to take out one memory without erasing a ton of others. You might even forget your own self."

"I'm not hexing him. I'm leaving." Vestra said. She pointed the wand at herself.

"Wait," Eric said. Vestra stopped and waited for him

to speak. "I didn't mean I wanted to forget you. I just meant..." Eric ran a hand through his hair. He was at a loss for words.

"While you figure that out, I'll take the paint can to the police station." Vestra held her hand out, and Alice handed her the spray paint can. Vestra waved her wand and disappeared.

The sound of wood creaking caught everyone's attention as Eric fell onto the other stool next to his grandmother. He sat in a daze. Zade and Puck exchanged a glance.

"We won't tell, right?" Zade said.

Puck sighed. "Yeah, we won't say anything."

"I remember," Mrs. Kinjo said to herself. Everyone looked at the old woman on the stool. Mrs. Kinjo looked thoughtful. After a few seconds, she said, "My husband met a man like that in Europe. He claimed to know about an ancient stone that could give a man magical abilities. When my husband met him, he had developed dementia, so no one believed him."

"That man, he had a stone he gripped before he disappeared," Alice said. Somewhere in her memory, she had heard something about these relics. It was probably something she'd heard from one of Mrs. Kinjo's many stories about her husband, the Professor of Anthropology.

It didn't seem so mysterious or intriguing to Puck or Zade as it was to Alice.

Puck said, "What I saw was a common charmed stone. They sell them at the thrift shop."

Alice could guess what a charmed stone was based

on context but would have liked a little clarity. She was grateful when Eric asked the question instead of her. "What's a charm stone?"

"A *charmed* stone is just a stone that holds magic," Zade said.

Surprisingly, Mrs. Kinjo added to Zade's explanation. "One spell only— for the holder of the stone to use or to curse the wearer."

"That's right," Puck said, "But how does an Untalented know that?" Vestra crossed her arms and looked at Alice.

"Are you telling them our secrets?" Zade asked.

"No," Alice said. At least that was honest.

"Secrets slip, but not from Alice," Mrs. Kinjo said, she had a twinkle in her eye as she looked at Alice.

"If you can't get a secret from her, try her cat," Puck said.

Alice's eyes widened. Naveed had told him something! She looked around for Naveed, who was not in the cat bed Alice had gotten for him and placed behind the counter. That traitor!

"What does he mean?" Zade asked.

Eric, Zade, and Mrs. Kinjo all looked at Alice. Unlike the others, Mrs. Kinjo was smiling. After a few seconds, Mrs. Kinjo broke into laughter.

"Kurrimaya, black cat. They are smart. They know everything," Mrs. Kinjo said.

Alice said, "Right. Um, Zade, you need to get to A Witch's Thrift Shop. Your sister's interview is probably over, and I'm sure your mom is looking for you. Puck—"

"Let me guess: You and I need to talk?" Puck asked.

"Yeah," Alice said.

"Go ahead, we're closed," Eric said. He walked over to his grandmother and reached to take her hand.

"No, you take what time you need to pull yourself together, then reopen the shop. Alice will walk me upstairs. Won't you?"

Eric knew better than to protest, but he jumped off the bench like he might run out of the place. Alice winced. She gave him a pitying look, but she walked to Mrs. Kinjo's side as requested.

"Of course, I'll help. Puck, will you—"

"Yep. See you in a while," Puck answered before Alice finished asking the question.

Alice took Mrs. Kinjo's hand and guided her to the back of the store. As they walked up the steps, Mrs. Kinjo squeezed Alice's hand. She began speaking in a soft voice.

"They think I know nothing. I don't know everything, but I know enough," Mrs. Kinjo said.

They stopped at the top step. Despite having more than enough money, the Kinjo's apartment was a humble assortment of old, mismatched furniture. Alice led Mrs. Kinjo to the brown, fabric recliner. Mrs. Kinjo sat slowly. She did not let Alice's hand go, so Alice had to sit on the ottoman beside her.

"My husband knew your father, Alice. I know he had magic," Mrs. Kinjo said.

"Why didn't you tell me?" Alice asked.

"Mr. Kinjo told me once that your father did not want you to know."

"Because I'm not like him. He was a wizard. You can't let anyone else know, but I do not have any magic." Tears began to fill Alice's eyes.

Mrs. Kinjo always kept a handkerchief in her sweater pocket. She pulled it out and gave it to Alice. As she did so, she said, "I don't know everything. But I do know that all people are talented in some way. And, I suspect, all of us are gifted with a little magic of our own. I'm sure you'll find yours, Alice."

Alice dried her eyes and hugged Mrs. Kinjo. She was wrong, but her heart was in the right place. Alice had no magic, but she loved the old woman for saying so, and, somewhere deep inside Alice, she hoped against all the odds that maybe it was true.

"Thank you," Alice said, and then she walked back down the stairs, past the empty shop, and out the door. She didn't see Eric anywhere, but she was sure he'd be all right. He just needed time. Puck had no such excuse.

"Puck!" Alice called out, but he was nowhere in sight.

Worse, there was no sign of Naveed. Once again, that unruly jinn had disobeyed orders. Next time, Alice would make it an official wish that he stay in place. More and more, she was beginning to understand how having a jinn was more a nuisance than a blessing.

When she saw him and Puck again, she'd give them both a piece of her mind. Unless Puck told on her. Then a part of Alice's mind would be taken: her memories.

TEN

Lost and Found

Alice did not go home. Half-way to her apartment, she got it in her mind to text Belinda. Taking the card from her back pocket, Alice entered the number and wrote a simple text:

"When are you free to meet?"

Seconds later, the text pinged back:

"Looking at the pictures now. Found something. Come and see."

When Alice got to her apartment building, she went straight up to the top level. At the third door to the right, she rang the buzzer.

"Door's open," Belinda called out.

Alice entered into a room that looked much like a studio. The layout was the same as her own apartment, but she wouldn't have guessed it at first glance.

Belinda's living room was set up with large lights angled against lifelike backgrounds. Three chairs sat in the corner. All the way pushed against the back of the kitchen island was a couch and a coffee table. There was no tv, but a ton of magazines on the table, all about photography and drawing. The wall was covered with photographs of Magic Row.

The camera on the table by the door was an old-fashion film camera, but Alice didn't see a dark room. Belinda must have developed them by magic, Alice supposed. Besides the photographs, there were also drawings. Alice moved closer for a better look.

The buildings in the drawings were similar to those on Magic Row, had names just off the real ones. Readings & Sons instead of Readings and Co., Witch's Brew Café instead of Witch's Brew Bakery, even Vestra's suggested title *"Thrifty Witch"* replaced the name A Witch's Thrift Shop. It was like staring at an alternate version of Magic Row.

The last one Alice saw was a freshly painted picture of Merlin's Shadow. Flames engulfed the top of the building. It was a strange image to draw and so realistic it made Alice's spine tingle. Was it a warning or a threat?

"Here we are, hot tea always calms me after a day like this," Belinda said. She bridged the distance from the kitchen to the living room carrying a tray, which she lowered for Alice. There was a simple, white, ceramic teapot and two cups filled with a milky white tea that smelled of chamomile.

Alice took a cup, saying, "Thank you. Your drawings and photos are wonderful."

"Thank you, but the drawings aren't mine."

"Why did you draw different-" Alice began, but Belinda spoke simultaneously.

"The pictures I took of the auction—oh, sorry," Belinda said.

"No, go ahead. What about the pictures?" Alice asked.

"The pictures I took of the auction table seemed exactly the same before and after. It took me a while to spot the difference."

"Something should have been missing," Alice said.

"Yes, I found it– after a while." Belinda set down the tea tray and sat on the sofa. She shuffled through some photos scattered on the coffee table.

"Here it is," Belinda pulled a picture out of the pile and placed it between them.

Alice bent over it, squinting. Belinda opened a drawer in the coffee table and took out a magnifying glass, which she held over the auction table in one picture. Belinda pointed.

"There, do you see it?" she asked.

"The table is empty there. Try moving the magnifying glass," Alice said.

"It's in the right place. It's an empty spot." Belinda lifted the magnifying glass to her lips and whispered something onto the glass. It came away fogged from her breath, but the fog did not disappear in seconds as it would normally. This time when they looked through the clouded glass, there was an object in the frame. Belinda continued, "Whatever you thought was taken, must have been taken before I could snap a picture of it. The secret was spotting the empty space and using magic to reveal what was there before."

"What is it?" Alice asked.

"Look closer and see," Belinda said.

Alice peered into the glass. Now she could see a ribbon, something that looked like a bracelet. It had a stone wrapped in a net, similar to the one the vandal was wearing, but in blue. It was short to be a necklace, though for all Alice knew it might have the power to magically grow around the neck of the wearer, to change color or anything like it. Could it have been the same one worn by the culprit? But why would Titania give something like that to an Untalented vandal?

"A charmed stone?" Alice said.

"Yep, a car charm, which makes no sense. Why would anyone want to steal a good luck charm?" Belinda said.

Alice scratched her head. "Doesn't a charmed stone hold one spell—any spell?'

"Oh, I didn't think of that. Most people just use a luck enhancement spell —which, those don't even work half the time, but it's the thought that counts. I guess some people do use it for other spells. But what kind?"

"How about the kind you placed on Tom's card?" Alice asked.

Belinda's jaw dropped. "Someone used a charmed stone to allow a vandal into mage-protected territory? Who would do such a thing?"

"Maybe the stone wasn't meant for the vandal, it just got into the wrong hands." Alice shrugged.

She told Belinda about the vandal in Magic Row, his brownish-red hair, his hood and painter's mask, and the amber stone around his neck. When all was said and done, Belinda sipped her chamomile tea and stared at the picture.

"But the stone in the picture is blue."

"Couldn't it change color?"

"Change color, how? Last I heard, topaz is topaz, amber is amber, amethysts are amethysts, stones don't just change into other stones," Belinda said. She pointed to the picture, "Plus, this is a car charm. I guess you to take it off and strap it to a necklace, but didn't you say this was on the auction table before the rock was thrown into the shop? How did the vandal get into Magic Row before they took the charm?"

This time Alice took a long sip of her tea and thought deeply. Belinda was right. They weren't just different color stones, they were different stones. Whoever threw the rock had thrown it too soon after Titania had left the shop. She wouldn't have had time to help him. Titania didn't see the type to help common vandals either. Something more was going on here.

"Maybe the charm doesn't have to do with the vandalism," Alice said.

"Then who would take it? Don't say 'Tom' again," Belinda said.

"No, it wasn't Tom." Alice held the warm cup in her hands and stared at the photograph.

"You said that like you know who. Did you see the theft?" Belinda asked.

"No," Alice said quickly.

Alice couldn't accuse Titania. Plus, she couldn't think of why she would take the charm off the police auction table. It was evidence in a previous police case.

Was Titania somehow involved in a police case in the past?

"Maybe it has to do with an old police case. They probably have a record of the items in the auction at the station," Alice said to herself.

"I could ask Tom, too," Belinda said.

"Tom, how would he have a police file?" Alice asked, recalling at that moment that he was a criminal attorney.

"He didn't realize at the time that many of his clients were mages, but the magical community tends to stick to their own. Many knew he was Liza's husband, so they naturally trusted him more when it came to court battles. He's only one of two lawyers Urbana's mages use, and the other is retired now."

"For someone who doesn't like magic, he's really involved in the community."

"Mmhmm, that's part of what scared him when he found out magic was real." Belinda said.

"Apparently he's not so scared anymore," Alice said.

"What do you mean?" Belinda asked.

"He showed up at A Witch's Thrift Shop after everyone left."

"Really?" Belinda bit her lip.

Alice turned to face her. "Don't worry, I'd never tell anyone that you allowed him access. I don't think anyone would tell. I mean, I don't know Tom, but I'm sure…"

"Tom would never say anything," Belinda said.

"Then you have nothing to worry about." Alice set down her tea, adding, "I should get going. Look, if you really want to make sure no one finds out about Tom's card, we should probably keep this whole business with the necklace between us for now. It might not even be a big deal, so I'd rather do a little digging of my own before getting anyone else involved."

Belinda smiled. "Tom might be able to help with that. And I won't say anything. I'm good with secrets, though I'm even better when I'm occupied in my art. Do you think you could let me do a photoshoot of Many Treasures sometime? It's a hobby of mine, taking pictures of all the stores in Magic Row."

Alice did not want to make a promise about letting another witch into Many Treasures, but Belinda had good intentions, and a few pictures seemed harmless. "Sure, thanks for everything," Alice said.

"Anytime. It's my pleasure to help a…level 7 or 8? Some of the mages are saying you're a level 9, is that true?"

Belinda was prying for information. More and more witches and wizards had been subtly asking about Alice's magical abilities. She didn't want to lie, but she wasn't sure how to keep avoiding the topic. She tried deflecting again.

"I'm nowhere near a level 9," Alice said, laughing. It was a nervous laughter, but she hoped Belinda wouldn't notice her anxiety—or that she wasn't going to answer. "Thanks again," Alice said, walking to the door.

As she left, Alice considered her next steps. If she took her concerns to the police, it might raise suspicions against Titania, and Ron would not appreciate accusations against his sister. Tom seemed like the best bet.

If Alice was honest, she also wanted to meet Tom. Liza was becoming a good friend, and Alice didn't want to see her or her kids hurt. It would be good to know more about the man who had broken their hearts.

But Alice wouldn't see him tonight. He might still be with Liza or with the kids. Their family reunion did not need Alice's interference. She wished them well.

And she wished that Naveed would stop disappearing on her. Enough was enough. She was worried now that her all-powerful jinn-cat had been kidnapped by a teenage wizard. It was time to go looking for him.

ELEVEN

Found Out

A fter hours of searching, Alice returned home exhausted. Every nook and cranny from Main Street to the broader Urbana area held no sign of a genie in the form of a cat. The next time she saw him, she would make it a wish that he had to return to her whenever she called.

Luckily, the next time she saw him was seconds after turning the key on her front door. There he was in cat-form, laid out on the rug beside the TV set. His eyes were fixed on the screen.

"Good to see you haven't been kidnapped," Alice said as she shut the door.

Naveed didn't look at her. He was barely blinking at the screen. Alice wasn't even sure he was watching anything instead of just ignoring her.

"All right. What is wrong with you? And why are you still in cat form?" Alice asked.

A sound to her left made her jump. The fridge door shut, and Puck set two soda cans down on the counter.

Puck's smile was more than amused as he scratched his head.

"Yeah, why would a *cat* still be a cat?" Puck asked. "Funny question, isn't it?"

"Puck, what are you doing here?" Alice asked.

"I was going to wait outside a Witch's thrift shop, but your *cat* said you had some leftover pizza." He pointed to two plates in the sink.

"Sorry, Alice," Naveed said, rather he meowed, and Alice understood.

"What are you talking about?" Alice asked.

Puck pointed at the cat. "He's not a normal cat. He's just like Hex. Don't deny it. I saw the two of them talking." Puck opened the soda can and took a swig.

Alice crossed her arms and narrowed her eyes at Naveed. In cat-form, Naveed rolled his eyes, and then he transformed into a jinn. Alice flinched as he walked toward her, as a big blue man he was far more intimidating than a cat. And if she had lost control of her lamp…this wasn't good.

Alice uncrossed her arms and backed up. "What are you doing?" She asked.

Naveed raised a hand. Puck tossed him a can of soda, and Naveed caught it without looking. He snapped the can open and drank. He gave a long contented, "Ah," when he was done.

Wiping his mouth with his forearm, Naveed said, "It's no use hiding it, Puck saw me talking with Hex. He knows I'm a real familiar."

"A *real* familiar?" Alice asked. Naveed lowered his

head and raised his brows at Alice. "Right, a familiar. You and Hex are both…familiars," Alice said.

"I knew it! I knew they still existed. They're real, *actual* familiars, like the old days, not like the ones witches and wizards keep today. It's so *stupid* teaching pets simple magic tricks and calling them *familiars* like they're the real thing." Puck said.

"Puck. You can't tell anyone," Alice said.

Puck stopped. "Are you a warlock?" Puck asked with his chin raised and eyes threatening to turn her in for sure.

"What? No." Alice said. She knew from context and from what Celeste had told her that warlocks were witches and wizards who broke magic laws. Alice longed for last week when all she worried about was being identified as an Untalented. This was just too much. "Of course I'm not a warlock, how could you ask me that?"

Puck relaxed. "I figured you weren't. But why hide it? Isn't it wonderful to have a real familiar? I mean, you have to be a level 9 like Baz. That carries some respect."

Naveed gave a deep-throated chuckle. Alice frowned at him. To Puck, she said, "I don't want the attention. Please, Puck, you have to promise."

Puck studied her. "Are you running away, too?"

Alice cocked her head. "What do you mean?"

Puck gripped the soda can. His eyes shifted from Alice to the island counter, and he stared a long while. Then he lifted the can and grinned as if giving cheers. "Never mind, you don't want to talk about it. I get that. I'll keep your secret on one condition."

Alice sat on the barstool opposite Puck. "What do you want?"

"A cozy couch and a nice living space works for me."

"Where are you living now?" Alice asked.

"Here and there. Mostly in abandoned places."

"You don't have a home?"

"I'm hoping I do now. It's just temporary while I get my act together."

"You're going to get a job or go to school or something?"

"No, my act. My magic show. I've got a few auditions, and I'm going to do a real show in a few weeks. If all goes well, I'll have some regular gigs, and then it's easy money after that."

"Money is not as easy to make as you think. And how real are we talking for these shows?" Alice said.

Puck rolled his eyes, "I'm not going to do anything that would make the Untalented suspicious. And I'd like to have Naveed in the show if you'll let him."

"I do not need Alice's permission." Naveed held his head eye.

Both Puck and Alice raised eyebrows. Naveed's shoulders slumped a little. He looked at Alice. "I believe you to be fair and honest."

"You want to do a magic show?" Alice asked.

"Tricking humans may be diverting," Naveed said.

Alice put her hands up, "Fine. Go ahead."

"So, I can stay?" Puck asked.

Alice had so many reasons Puck couldn't stay. For one, her tiny apartment was already crowded with

Naveed staying out of his lamp at all times. Secondly, it would be a lot harder to hide the fact that she was Untalented or to have private conversations with Naveed about how to keep pretending to be a witch. Alice tried hard not to consciously acknowledge the third reason —that Puck wasn't completely trustable, but then, she was trusting him with more than one secret now, wasn't she?

The answer hit Alice, and she walked back to the door, saying, "I have a much better idea. Come on."

TWELVE

Safe Spaces

_____

The lights were still on downstairs in Many Treasures. Eric and Vestra were sitting on the barstools behind the cash register laughing when Alice walked in with Puck and Naveed, in cat form, in tow. It was nice to see that Eric had calmed down and reopened the shop. It was also a little disconcerting that Vestra's hand was resting just above Eric's knee.

"Are we interrupting something?" Alice asked, noting that the two were alone in close quarters.

Eric sat up straighter. "No." He traced Alice's eye to Vestra's hand and promptly stood up. "I'll go close the shop."

Vestra leaned forward and watched Eric walk away. When her view was blocked by the counter, she looked. "I was just about to ask Eric over to my place," Vestra said.

"You were?" Eric and Alice said in unison. Eric gave Alice an annoyed look and continued to shut off the sign and lock the door. Alice didn't mean to sound so surprised. Eric was fit and fine-looking, but he'd seen the inside of a library a million times and a woman's apartment...maybe none. It's not like Alice kept track of Eric's love life. Still, she did see enough of him every day to know that Vestra's interest was an anomaly in an otherwise dull daily routine.

Vestra gazed at Eric. "I told you I wanted to show you the rooftop garden at my apartment building. You said it sounded like a perfect place to do your stargazing."

"You meant tonight?" Eric asked.

Vestra nodded.

"Hold on, Eric, I need to speak with you—just for a minute," Alice said.

"Can't it wait?" Eric asked, not taking his eyes off Vestra.

"Not really, sorry," Alice said.

"It's OK." Vestra got up and went to her purse. She opened her wallet and took a small picture out of it. Taking a pen off the counter, she flipped the photo over and wrote something on the back. Then, Vestra held the picture between her hands. A light flashed between her fingers.

She handed the photo to Eric, saying, "This is an invitation. You hold it in both hands, read the location I wrote on the back, and the photo will take you there."

Eric accepted the card with a wide smile. "I'll see you in a few minutes," he said.

"Always good to see you, Alice," Vestra said, still looking at Eric.

"Eric," Alice had to call his name twice to get his attention.

"Yeah, I'm listening," he said.

"I have to ask you and your grandmother a question," Alice asked.

"If it's: 'Do we forgive you for getting us involved in a magical community without our knowledge or permission,' the answer is yes. But we're still very annoyed with you."

Alice crossed her arms, "Your grandmother is not annoyed with me."

"All right, fine, *I* am."

"Really, because you didn't seem so upset with Vestra," Puck said.

Naveed chuckled, which was disconcerting coming from a cat. Mid-laugh, he meowed. Eric raised an eyebrow at Naveed but shook it off.

"Vestra and I talked it out. It's not her fault we have to pretend to be mages now, is it?"

"OK, sure, it's my fault, but I didn't mean to get either of you involved; it just kind of happened. And you have to admit that it hasn't been all bad."

Eric looked at the photo in his hand, "I guess not."

"Good, because I'm about to make your lives even better," Alice said, walking toward the staircase.

"She means worse," Puck said, following her upstairs.

"Wait, what do you mean worse?" Eric said. He sneezed as Naveed jumped on his shoulders, hitching a ride to the second floor.

Upstairs, the apartment smelled like fresh tomatoes,

cilantro, lemon, and the gentle tang of Sansho peppers. The table was set for three, possibly because Mrs. Kinjo had been expecting Vestra to stay for dinner. As Alice and Puck entered the apartment, Mrs. Kinjo looked out from the kitchen.

"Alice you are back, and who is this child you brought with you?" Mrs. Kinjo asked.

"His name is Puck. I brought him here to ask if he could stay," Alice said.

"Of course, the more guests, the better the dinner is enjoyed. Ah, good, Eric, come help me prepare the plates." Mrs. Kinjo said, waving Eric into the kitchen as he reached the top stair.

"You don't just mean dinner, do you?" Eric asked as he passed Alice and Puck.

"No," Alice said.

"I'll take the dinner," Puck said, walking briskly to the table.

Mrs. Kinjo and Eric together brought out four plates and another place setting. Eric went back into the kitchen and returned with another water glass. He set it on the table in front of Alice as she sat down.

"I can't stay, Baa-Baa," Eric said, not sitting with Alice and Puck.

Naveed took Eric's seat. Alice tried to get him to come down, to no avail. He just hissed and growled.

"Going to see the girl you've been chatting with all day instead of working?" Mrs. Kinjo asked.

Eric shrugged. "The shop was open. Anyway, she helped me understand more about the whole…magic thing, and I get it now," he said.

Puck and Alice exchanged glances. "You *'get'* magic now?" Alice asked.

"He gets the girl, what else is there to get?" Puck asked.

Alice shot a frown in Puck's direction. He focused his attention on the plate. The taco rice was still steaming, and he closed his eyes to take in the aroma of the salsa topping.

"And this girl will have dinner ready for you?" Mrs. Kinjo asked as she set the plates down.

Eric put a hand to the back of his neck and eyed the dish. "No, I don't think so."

Mrs. Kinjo pulled the plate toward Naveed. "Too bad," said Mrs. Kinjo. Then she went back into the kitchen.

Eric put the photo on the table and took the plate before Naveed could dig into it. "Maybe just a few bites," Eric said, earning the wrath of the cat-jinn, Naveed, who hissed and bared his teeth. His hiss became a growl as Naveed moved him from the chair to the floor.

"Naveed," Alice whispered. Naveed's black eyes turned to Alice. Mrs. Kinjo reentered with another plate, this one plastic for Naveed. His anger subsided. Mrs. Kinjo set the dish down in front of Naveed and petted his head.

"So, about Puck," Alice began. "I was hoping he could stay with you for a little while."

"Just a few weeks," Puck added.

Eric looked at Puck, then his grandmother, then Naveed. "As long as it's not the cat." He pointed at

Naveed with his fork. Naveed hissed. Alice gave him another stern look, and he went back to silently enjoying his meal. Eric did the same.

"He goes to school?" Mrs. Kinjo asked.

Alice looked at Puck. "Do you?" she asked.

Puck gave Alice a side-eyed grimace and looked more respectfully at Mrs. Kinjo, "I'm working on my magic act," he said.

Eric nearly choked. He took a gulp from his glass of water and said, "You mean magic shows are real?"

"Relax, Eric. Those are still fake as ever," Alice said.

"Mine will be too, at least I won't do anything that people will think is real."

Eric raised an eyebrow but did not say anything further.

Mrs. Kinjo's attention remained on her point. "How old are you?" she asked.

"Nearly seventeen," Puck replied.

"Not nearly old enough to be performing magic for a living. Young men in this house go to school until they are at least eighteen," Mrs. Kinjo said.

Alice smiled, silently taking another bite and letting Mrs. Kinjo do her own magic. Her plan was working. If anyone could set Puck straight, it was Mrs. Kinjo.

Puck shook his head. "No way, I'm not staying here if I have to give up my magic."

"You can do magic. In fact, you can use your magic to help out around the apartment. You just have to educate yourself. I don't live with fools."

"My grandmother calls me a fool about three times a week," Eric whispered to Alice, not soft enough.

"Because wise people know that books don't have everything in them. You have to leave the classroom sometime and live."

"Which is it? Learning or living? It sounds like you don't like either." Puck said.

"I like both. Alice knows the right balance—at least, I think she's learning now."

"What do you mean, Hamee?"

"You were going to waste your life in a museum. But now you found some magic in your life. And your choosing to live with that knowledge—even if it's dangerous."

"That's what I'm doing. I'm choosing the dangerous life," Puck grinned.

"A stupid life. You don't choose danger because it's dangerous," Mrs. Kinjo said.

"How is it stupid for me to choose a dangerous life and not for Alice?"

"Someone explain it to the boy," Mrs. Kinjo said.

"Someone explain it to me," said Eric.

Alice rolled her eyes. She pushed her plate back and turned to Puck. Looking him straight in the eyes, she said, "Puck, I don't know whether you ran away or what might have happened to bring you to Magic Row, but I don't think you'd choose a dangerous life if you could. And I think you're smart enough to know a good deal when you see it. Mrs. Kinjo is offering you a chance at a normal life. Do you really want to pass it up just because you think it's braver to be on your own?"

"Braver?" Eric asked. He laughed. "You may have it easy here with the meals and the free room and board, but just try testing my grandmother's patience. She will push you until you're top of your class at school and the number one magic act in the country. Trust me, it's braver to stay."

Puck stared at his plate. "Can I think about it?" Puck asked.

Naveed stopped eating and looked up at Alice. Alice looked at Eric, who shrugged. Mrs. Kinjo squinted her eyes at Puck and leaned forward.

"Do you like the food?" Mrs. Kinjo asked.

"Yes," Puck said.

"And the house is nice, yes?"

"Yes, ma'am," Puck said.

"Good. Think about that," she said, and she began her meal.

"I think that means you can stay," Alice said. Naveed seemed satisfied with the answer. He resumed eating.

"Well, I've got to go," Eric said, pushing aside his empty plate. He reached for the photo, which Alice noticed he'd placed face down. She made a note of the address: Green Houses Plaza. She knew the place. That entire side of town had been falling into disrepair.

The Green Houses were once a beautiful site in Urbana, a group of apartments and condos separated by gardens and greenhouses that were now dilapidated structures with a few plants and expired permits. One of the buildings and several of the greenhouses were in the middle of restoration. They had been under construction for several years without progress. To be fair, the occupied buildings were still elegant, but nowhere near the splendor they once had.

Eric excused himself and took the photo, which Alice could now see was a picture of Vestra by the window in her apartment. The sun lit up a greenhouse in the background. It was beautiful. Alice was sure the rooftop garden would be just as nice and that neither Eric nor Vestra would notice it. Eric walked to his room and came out carrying his telescope.

"So, how does this work?" He held the photo in his hands.

"Hold it and read the address," Puck said.

"Like this?" Eric held the card, read the apartment number, and promptly disappeared.

"He forgot his telescope," Puck said.

Alice stifled a laugh and said, "I think he'll be OK without it."

Alice spent the rest of the night with Puck and Mrs. Kinjo. Naveed had stuffed himself with two plates of taco rice and dozed on the sofa. Mrs. Kinjo brought out old family photos, many of which included Alice.

"This one is special," Mrs. Kinjo said.

She moved the book to Alice's lap and pointed. It was a much younger Alice, in the first year she'd met the Kinjos when Eric's parents had still been alive. There were balloons all around, and Eric was smiling in a cap and gown.

"Eric's high school graduation," Alice said. Her smiled turned to a frown. Eric's parents died in a car accident shortly after.

"Why does it make you sad?" Puck asked.

"It shouldn't," said Mrs. Kinjo. "It was a great accomplishment and one that made his parents proud."

"They died." Puck was a smart kid to figure that out. He asked, "How?"

"It does not matter how we die. It matters how we live. Eric may work too hard, but he's living up to his potential. His parents still see that now, and they are proud. Are you living up to your potential?" Mrs. Kinjo asked Puck.

Puck got up. He walked to the telescope and began fiddling with it. He might have been avoiding Mrs. Kinjo's question, but she didn't relent. She got up, slowly with her cane, and began showing him how to work the telescope properly. As they talked, Alice peered at the photo.

In it, she was wearing a necklace she remembered vaguely, but hadn't worn in years. It was a long rope-chain with a stone hung inside a net. It was a purple stone, an amethyst— a charmed stone! Now she remembered it. Her mother had given it to her before she'd died. She'd told her to wear it always.

Alice had done so for many years. She had treasured it all through her childhood, but the older she got, the more her memories faded. Eventually, she started wearing other jewelry and the charmed stone less and less until somehow she'd stopped altogether. What had happened to the necklace? Alice suddenly felt a sort of panic at the thought of it being lost. It was strange how something in her childhood still mattered so much to her.

Alice didn't even wear jewelry anymore, except for a rare occasion. Would it still be in the old jewelry box at home? Alice wondered.

She closed the album, ready to go home and search for the missing treasure. When she looked up, Mrs. Kinjo was nowhere in sight. Alice pet Naveed's head, saying, "Come on, time to go."

He rose lazily, blinking several times to wake himself up. He jumped off the couch, and Alice called out her good-byes. Mrs. Kinjo appeared from the hallway, chuckling.

"Where's Puck?" Alice asked.

Mrs. Kinjo shook her head. "He's on the fire escape, looking at the stars- just like Eric. It's a good place to think.

Alice smiled. "I remember. Eric used to go there all the time whenever he had to make a difficult decision."

"Not just difficult decisions, Eric would stay out there when he was sad or worried or upset. That boy is feeling all of those things. I think that's why he ran away. He's looking for a safe place."

"We all have our safe places," Alice said to herself.

For Alice, strange as it sounded, her safe space had been visiting her parents' graves. Suddenly, she recalled wearing the necklace to her parents' gravesite. She used to visit when she was scared and upset. If Mara hadn't been kidnapped, if something scared her, the way Puck was feeling scared and all those emotions Mrs. Kinjo mentioned, could she have run for a safe space?

It was possible. If it was true, it meant Alice could find her. All she had to do was figure out what Mara considered her safe space and get there before whatever she was running from caught up with her.

"Thank you, Hamee," Alice said. She opened the

door and let Naveed out first. Then she turned around and added, "You've been a big help, both to Puck and to me."

THIRTEEN

Blest and Cursed

Alice had no intention of interrupting Eric's date. All she wanted to do was check out the Green Houses Plaza. She had a hunch that Mara had a safe space just like Eric did, somewhere in one of the abandoned greenhouses perhaps. She asked Naveed to take her to the top of the tallest building. How was she to know that the tallest tower was Vestra's apartment building?

Alice heard giggling and caught a glimpse of Vestra and Eric lying on a lawn chair. Vestra's head rested on Eric's chest as the two stared up at the stars. Eric, in classic *"Eric"* fashion, pointed out the constellations above. Alice was reasonably sure Vestra was far less interested in Orion's belt than in Eric's.

"He's way too sweet for her," Alice said, apparently to no one. "Naveed? Where are you?" she whispered.

Naveed hadn't seen the cozy pair on the rooftop. Thinking the area was clear, he had proceeded to transform himself into his jinn form. He was scouring the roof for a better view of the greenhouses when Vestra caught sight of him.

"Oh, Eric, we're not alone," Vestra said. She popped out of her chair as if embarrassed, though Alice couldn't see any reason for embarrassment. Eric seemed confused about it, too. He stood up, following her lead, and stuck his hand out.

"I'm Eric Kinjo," he said.

Naveed did not shake his hand. Vestra smiled and said in a flirty tone of voice, "I'm Vestra Starr, I don't think we've met before."

Naveed said nothing for a minute, and Alice debated going out to his aid or stopping him from using his magic on the pair. Alice would have a hard time explaining to Eric and Vestra why she was on the roof and an even harder time explaining about having a jinn with her. Thankfully, in the dark night, Naveed's blue skin tone looked black, so it wasn't evident that he was a jinn. And he didn't try to perform any kind of magic on them, so they were both safe.

In his deep throaty voice, Naveed said, "I'm looking for Mara Blest."

Vestra paled. "Why?" she asked, leaning into Eric.

"I am concerned for her safety," Naveed said.

"Oh, are you the officer?" Vestra asked.

"What officer?" Alice whispered to herself. Naveed's silence prompted Vestra to clarify.

"Don't worry, Mara told me not to tell anyone, so I didn't. But I know all about the accident and the officer who helped her. Does her disappearance have anything to do with that?"

Naveed said nothing, prompting more nervous speech from Vestra, "You must have heard that she's gone, right?"

Eric spoke up, "What's going on? Is this about the thrift shop employee?"

Vestra nodded, not taking her eyes off Naveed. Fear was casting its shadow in her eyes. Naveed had a way of doing that to people.

"When I say I know all about the accident, I don't mean I know everything. I just know that Mara was scared about going to jail and that an officer helped her to…I don't know exactly…just that she felt like she would have gone to jail without your help. That's all she told me."

"What accident?" Eric asked.

"Shh. Just a car accident," Vestra said quickly.

If Naveed had been someone more threatening, Alice would have agreed with Vestra about Eric not asking more questions. But, since they weren't in any real danger, Alice wanted nothing more than for Eric to keep prying for more information. With Vestra scared as she was, it didn't look like she was going to say anything else.

After a minute of silence, Naveed said, "Do you know where Mara is now?"

Vestra did not say anything aloud. She only shook her head. Naveed eyed her a while, and she sank further into Eric's side. Eric held her tight, not asking any more questions. Finally, Naveed bowed and walked back toward Alice in the shadows.

When Naveed reached Alice, she whispered, "Wait,

go back and ask her if there's a place around here that Mara might choose to hide out, like a safe space or something."

"I don't think I need to go back," Naveed said.

"Just once, just to ask her that."

"Alice," Naveed said.

"Naveed, I wish," Alice began.

Naveed put his hands on Alice's shoulder and turned her body to face the edge of the building. When Alice turned back in protest, Naveed gently turned her chin.

"Look," Naveed said.

She looked in the direction he had pointed her. It took Alice a second to spot it, but there was a dim light coming from one of the taped-off greenhouses below. It was a construction area at ten o'clock at night, so the light was unexpected. It was worth checking out.

Alice gave Naveed her hand and made a different wish. "Take me there," she said.

Naveed clasped her arm, and they made the shift through spaces. It always made Alice feel queasy for a minute. Her eyes had to adjust to the dying shrubbery and dim light. The musty smell and thick air in the place did not help. Alice fought the sick sensation in her stomach and let go of Naveed.

"You should change," Alice whispered.

Naveed shrank into his cat-jinn form. Alice couldn't see anyone around them, but her whisper must have been overheard in the tight space. The sound of a pot clanging came from around the row of browning plants.

"Who's there?" a shaky voice asked.

"Mara?" Alice said as she walked around the row of plant holders.

Just around the corner, a wide-eyed, purple-haired woman stared back at them, frozen with fear. Only her eyes moved as she glanced at the nearby table. A hand shovel, shears, and a gnarled twig rested three feet from the woman. Two weeks ago, Alice would have thought the twig was just a broken branch. Now she knew it was a wand.

Naveed crept forward like a tiger stalking his prey. Alice gave him a stern look, so that he stopped his advance. Still, he growled, keeping his shoulders up and claws out, just in case.

Mara eyed the wand and leaned toward the counter. Putting both hands up in as non-threatening a manner as possible, Alice called her name again. Mara hesitated, though she could have jumped for her wand at any moment.

"I'm unarmed, and I'm not a police officer," Alice said. Whatever Mara's reason was for hiding out, it had sounded like it had something to do with the law. It seemed right for Alice to reassure her that she wasn't with the police.

Mara kept her eyes on the table as she talked. "Then what are you doing here?" Mara asked.

Alice wondered the same thing. She thought she was saving a spooked young witch. Without really thinking about it, Alice had jumped into confronting a possible criminal.

"I'm here to help you. Liza is worried about you," Alice said.

Mara's expression softened. "I didn't mean to worry anyone," she said.

"A lot of people care about you, Mara. All of Urbana's mage community is on the lookout for you."

Mara looked at her feet as if deciding whether to run. She glanced between Alice and the door. "Are you going to turn me in?" she asked.

"Turn you in to whom?" Alice asked.

"You know. The police," Mara said.

"For what, Mara? What did you do?" It dawned on Alice just then, "Are you the one who threw the rock into A Witch's Thrift Shop?"

Mara swallowed, then burst out, "No, that's exactly why I'm running. He's dangerous…I thought I could trust him, but…he has power now, and he's showing his true self to Magic Row…" Mara stopped herself. She looked sick, like if she said much more, she might vomit.

"Who do you mean?" Alice couldn't figure it out. Mara had said "he," so it couldn't be Celeste or Vestra. Surely, it wasn't Baz. He was powerful and owned most of Magic Row, but he hadn't suddenly gotten power or changed his personality. He had seemed shocked to learn about Mara's disappearance.

Mara seemed fine with everyone until the night she went missing— the night after Celeste told her about the police auction. Vestra had mentioned an officer that had helped Mara. Had that officer turned on her now?

"Mara, are you hiding from someone from the police station?" Alice asked.

Mara shook her head. "I've said too much already," she replied. She grabbed her wand and ran to the door.

"Wait, stop!" Alice said. Naveed readied himself to pounce, but Alice caught him in the air.

Mara turned sideways in the doorframe. "If you try to stop me, I'll hex you." Then she disappeared.

Naveed wriggled free of Alice's grasp and transformed back into his jinn-form. "Why did you stop me? I could have caught her," he said.

"She would have fought back."

"She couldn't harm me." Naveed had to cross his arms, puffing his chest up as if to prove his words.

Alice pinched the bridge of her nose, feeling the start of a migraine. "I know. I didn't want *you* to harm *her*," she said.

Naveed held an open palm toward the door, saying, "She's clearly a criminal, and she's getting away!"

"I don't think so, she was scared of someone. I don't think she's just running from the law. I think someone is chasing her."

"The mysterious "he." So, who is it?" Naveed asked.

"That's what we have to find out," Alice said.

FOURTEEN

Affairs and Answers

"Remind me why it is your duty to solve Mara's problem?" Naveed asked the next morning as they prepared to leave Alice's apartment early.

"It's the right thing to do," Alice said as she put on her jacket.

She couldn't be sure she was thinking straight since last nights' thoughts had all muddled together into a mind-numbing headache. Only Alice's feelings were clear to her. She felt an urgency to help. How she would do so for Mara, Magic Row, or even Liza or Baz, given her knowledge of the affair, remained a puzzle.

"Wouldn't the right thing be to take this information to the police?" Naveed asked.

"Not if someone at the police station is the one who is scaring her," Alice said.

"Then we should be trying to find out who at the station is threatening her, not going to some lawyer," Naveed said.

"I told you last night. Tom is a *criminal* lawyer. He's

handled many cases for the magic community around here. He might know something about the car accident or why Mara was scared about going to jail," Alice said.

"So, we see Tom and ask about Mara's case?"

"Exactly," Alice said.

"And this has nothing to do with Liza or the Willows children?" Naveed asked.

Alice thought about it. "It might be nice to get a sense of who Tom is and how he could have broken their hearts and left them," she said.

"You do not like this man," Naveed concluded.

"I can't say that until I meet him, which I'd like to do sometime this morning." Alice's tone was sharp.

Naveed, with a scowl, transformed into his cat form. Alice picked him up and scratched behind his ear. He meowed sharply. Alice couldn't help it, he was so cute as a his cat-jinn, but she stopped the scratching. "Sorry. I wish for you to take me to Tom's office, Naveed."

Alice's apartment faded away and was replaced with a hallway with marble floors and alabaster-colored walls. Though Tom seemed to dislike magic, he had surrounded himself with Belinda's paintings of Magic Row. As Alice walked down the hall, she almost felt like she was walking through the magical street.

The receptionist was a friendly, soft-spoken blonde woman who reminded Alice of Liza in some ways. Her name-tag read "Betsy," and she told Alice that Tom was unavailable.

"He's with a client. I could take a message." Betsy smiled. Her eyes flicked down to the floor where Naveed trotted to past the counter.

"Oh, there are no animals aloud," Betsy said in a *'we can't have that'* tone.

"Sorry about that." Alice followed Naveed. Before she could scoop him into her arms, he'd pushed Tom's office door open. The voices inside spilled into the hallway.

"It's been over for three years. You need to stay out of my life," came a male voice.

"You think I want you back? Get over yourself, Tom. I'm here because of Mara, she's using this against me, and if she takes me down, I'm taking you down with me. Then your happily ever after with your pretty little ex-wife goes out the window—if she'll even take you back."

"Titania," Tom said. He stopped. His eyes met Alice's in the doorway, and he froze.

Titania looked toward the door and gasped. Alice picked Naveed up in a hurry and stepped back. Betsy appeared in the doorway. She gripped Alice's elbow firmly.

"I'm sorry, sir; she went right past me," Betsy said.

"Get her out. I want no disruptions for at least the next half hour," Tom said.

Alice racked her brain for a response. She couldn't let them push her out now. She was just starting to put it all together. "I'm here to help," Alice said.

"Wait, let her in," Titania commanded.

Betsy looked at Tom. He frowned, then nodded. Alice pulled her elbow away, set Naveed back on the floor, and stepped inside. Betsy pulled the door closed behind her.

"What do you mean you're here to help?" Titania

asked.

Alice thought aloud, "You had an affair with Tom while he was still married. Mara found out. She blackmailed you into stealing the charmed stone from A Witch's Thrift Shop."

"You stole something?" Tom asked.

Titania ignored Tom. She crossed her arms and asked, "How exactly are you helping?"

Based on Titania's reaction, Alice's conclusions were right. She continued her train of thought. "I think Mara needed the stone to help her get out of trouble with the police somehow. If I know more about the situation, maybe I can help her, and she won't be desperate enough to blackmail you. Do you know why she would want the stone?" Alice asked.

"I wouldn't know the first thing about Mara. If you ask me, whatever she's accused of, she's guilty." Titania sat in the chair, crossing her legs first and her arms as she reddened to a shade close to the carpet. Tom leaned over his desk, bringing a hand to his chin.

Alice turned to Tom. "Did you handle a police case involving Mara Blest?"

He gave Alice a sharp look. "I can't divulge information about my cases."

"This information could get Mara off Titania's back."

Titania uncrossed her arms and sighed. "Give her the case file," she said.

Tom glanced between Titania and Alice. He turned around, opened a cherry wood filing cabinet, and, after a minute of searching, took out a case file. Tom set it on the desk and opened it, pulling it back defensively as Naveed jumped onto the counter.

Tom raised an eyebrow and looked at Alice, "Who is he?"

Titania rolled her eyes. "For mercy's sake, Tom, it's just a cat. Will you read the file?"

Tom shooed Naveed to the corner of the desk and held the case file up, blocking his view. Looking at Alice, Tom said, "I can only tell you what's public information. Three years ago, Mara's boyfriend, a man named Vaughn Hawkson, was in a car accident that left him severely injured. Foul play was suspected but never proven. Mara was a person of interest."

"That witch! She hexed the charmed stone. She wanted to get rid of the evidence," Titania said.

"Could a hex on the charmed stone cause an accident?" Alice said aloud.

"If the right hex is used. I thought you were a level nine," Titania looked Alice up and down.

Alice's shoulders tightened, and she folded her arms. Could it be as simple as Mara sabotaging the car with the charmed stone? "Why would Mara want to kill her boyfriend?" Alice asked aloud.

"The accident didn't kill him. Vaughn lost his memory and returned to his home country for recovery. He never pressed any charges."

"Now they have the police auction. She's worried a Talented officer like my brother will realize they never did an M-trace on the stone," Titania said.

"The case was closed. I'm not sure what an M-trace is, but cases like this where there was no fatality usually don't get reopened unless a major discovery comes to light," Tom said.

"Like the discovery of the charmed stone?" Alice asked.

Tom got up to put the file away, saying, "It's been in evidence for three years. The police knew they had the stone. I don't see why they'd suddenly take another look at it."

"Unless someone tipped them off," Alice said.

"I didn't," Titania said, holding her perfectly manicured fingernails to her heart. Alice didn't suppose Titania would care or know enough about Mara and her boyfriend to tip her brother off to any foul play.

"No, but someone did. Who was the officer involved in the case?"

Tom took a last look at the file before placing it back in the drawer, "An officer named Quinton Ramsey."

Alice's eyes widened. That was the same man who performed the M-trace on the stone in A Witch's Thrift Shop. Alice thanked Tom, called on Naveed to follow her, and turned to leave. She had to get to work at Many Treasures, but she knew where she would be going at the end of her shift.

Betsy gave Alice a snide smile as she passed her desk. Alice gave her a genuine "thank you" in return. She could hear Tom buzzing over the intercom. Seconds later, he was saying, "Send in my first client." Titania had left his office, but only to catch up with Alice and Naveed down the hallway.

"You won't tell Baz, will you?" Titania asked.

Alice turned around. Titania's honey-colored eyes

wavered, flaring in anger one second, and filling with fearful tears the next. Alice was almost moved to make a promise, but she couldn't quite commit.

"I'm not going to blackmail you or anything. You don't have to worry about that with me," Alice said.

"That's not a promise not to tell." Titania's look sharpened. Her eyebrows narrowed, and she lifted her wand.

Alice put her hands up. "Woah, Titania," Alice said.

"Get out your wand. Make a spell-sealed promise," Titania said.

"I'm not getting involved in your life, OK?" Alice said.

Naveed snarled. His growling caused Titania to step back. Titania relaxed her wand but put her hand to her forehead. She was almost shaking.

"But you already are involved. You know a secret that you have to promise to take to your grave. You have to promise you won't tell Baz."

Alice had to calm her down. "Didn't you and Baz just get engaged? I'm sure he won't care about a relationship you had with a divorcee three years ago.

"You don't understand—" Titania was nearly sobbing now— "The Delvaux's have their pride. If they knew I'd had an affair with a married man, Baz would never agree to marry me. The wedding would be called off."

"And you love him," Alice said. She didn't know why she said it. What business was it of hers? But something inside her knew that wasn't Titania's motivation—and she just had to know if all her accusations were true.

"Do you know what it's like to have your family count on you to get just one thing right after getting so many things wrong? Do you know how it feels to be the black sheep of your family?"

"I can't say that I do," Alice said.

"Of course not. You don't have a family." If Titania meant to wound Alice, she'd succeeded. Alice felt like she'd been hit in the heart with the worst kind of hex: one that wouldn't let her forget her own history.

Titania quickly pocketed her wand and looked away as a man in a business suit passed by. Even she knew not to be conspicuous among the Untalented. She walked closer to Alice. Alice got the hint and began walking down the hallway with her.

Titania's voice wavered. "I envy you. You don't have to hear about how you tarnish the family name or be compared to your perfect, hero brother." She smudged her makeup, wiping away angry tears.

Alice, Titania, and Naveed reached the end of the hallway. It was the end of the line, and Titania had Alice cornered, but Alice didn't feel the least bit threatened now.

She bent down and picked up Naveed.

"I can't make a spell-sealed promise, but I'm not interested in ruining your life. That's the best I can do," Alice said.

She did not wait for Titania's reaction. Instead, Alice looked down at Naveed, and he shifted the two of them to the downstairs of Many Treasures. This time the odd feeling in the pit of Alice's stomach wasn't just from magical travel. She didn't know why she hadn't just promised Titania that she wouldn't tell. Yes, she didn't have a wand, so she couldn't promise via magic, but she could have vowed through her own will power. It should have been easy. Baz's and Titania's relationship wasn't her business.

But she did feel that Liza and the Willows kids were her friends. And she wasn't sure she could keep the truth from Liza. *Poor Liza. Had she suspected Tom was having an affair with Titania? Had he known Titania was a witch at the time?* Alice wondered.

She could see why Tom was Titania's type. A handsome, high-earning lawyer gaining prominence in the magical community– even if he'd been unaware of it– must have been appealing to her. And, for Tom's part, anyone with eyes could see that Titania was attractive. It made a twisted kind of sense.

What Alice couldn't figure out was how they'd kept their affair secret. She supposed magic would make it easier for Titania to get away with sneaking in and out of Tom's office or home when Liza was away. But had anyone known? Obviously, Mara had found out, but she hadn't told Liza.

Was it disloyal for Alice to keep it from her? Or would it be cruel to bring up an affair from years ago? Alice needed time to think about it. Luckily, she had a few hours of work at Many Treasures before she would see Liza. Plus, she had a good excuse for canceling lunch with Liza and Celeste today: It was finally time to go to the police. At least, it was time for Alice to talk to Officer Quinton Ramsey.

FIFTEEN

Magical Crimes

The police station was on Main Street, about two blocks from Many Treasures, but Alice had, fortunately, had never had to go there before. She asked a young female officer at the front of the station for Officer Quinton Ramsey. After a quick phone call, the officer responded, "He'll see you in five minutes."

"Thank you," Alice said, and she sat down to wait beside an angry-looking man in a business suit furiously filling in a form. A woman in a tight fitted red dress and high heels sat on the other side of the room. She smacked her chewing gum and gave Alice a look that said, *"Mind your own business."*

Alice regretted not bringing Naveed, but a cat in a police station might be against the rules. It would at least draw unnecessary attention to herself. She could have called him an emotional support animal. A cat-jinn would definitely ease her emotions in a police station. Alice was relieved when she saw a familiar face.

"Well, hello. What brings you here? Is everything all right?" Ron asked.

Alice stood up. "I was hoping to speak to Officer Ramsey, but actually, I'm glad I bumped into you."

"Why is that?" Ron asked.

Alice took a deep breath. "Is there somewhere private we could speak?"

Ron walked Alice back to his desk. It was a cubicle, not the most private area. Alice was surprised he would talk about magic here.

"Maybe we should talk about this somewhere else since it involves...magic?" Alice mouthed the last word.

Ron smiled. "The station is hexed so that the Untalented can't pay attention when certain topics are discussed."

"They can't hear us?" Alice asked.

"They can hear it," Ron said, "But if they try to focus on it, they'll lose their train of thought and shrug it off. It's a standard confusion spell."

"Oh," Alice said, thinking of all the times she forgot what she was doing or thinking when she was out in public. Brain fog, she called it— a fitting name for a spell now that she thought of it.

But Alice wasn't just worried about the topic of magic. "What about Talented officers?" she asked.

"Are we hiding something from the Talented?" Ron asked.

Alice hesitated. "It's about Mara," she said. Alice wasn't sure where to start, but she continued, "Mara wasn't kidnapped, but she is running from someone.

She's terrified of a man, maybe a police officer from this station."

"An officer?" Ron asked.

Alice thought back to what Vestra had said on the rooftop. Without giving away her source, she said, "I think it's someone who might have helped her years ago but turned on her now."

"Someone who helped her with a coverup?" Ron asked.

"I didn't say that, but I do think it has something to do with her boyfriend's case," Alice said.

Ron nodded. "I looked into the boyfriend when Mara first disappeared." Ron looked something up on his computer. Alice couldn't see it but assumed it was Mara's boyfriend's case file. After a minute, Ron said, "Mara filed a complaint against him for allegedly abusive behavior, but she dropped it soon after. I thought he might be involved in her kidnapping, but he's not in the country now. He went home for recovery and never returned to the USA."

"But while he was here, he was abusive? Maybe this officer helped her get away from the boyfriend at the time. Maybe the officer even caused the accident. Mara said she thought she could trust him and that he turned on her."

Ron raised an eyebrow. "You spoke to Mara?"

Alice reddened. "I saw her briefly."

"Where?"

Alice shook her head. "I'd rather not say. She fled anyway, so I don't know where she is now. All I know is that she was scared—most likely of some kind of the officer. Ramsey was involved in the case, wasn't he? Could Mara be scared of him?"

"He worked the case, but before that, he doesn't seem to have known Mara personally. The boyfriend, Hawkson, applied to the police academy a month before the accident. If she was talking about some kind of officer, she might have meant him. I'll double-check on his whereabouts, but here's a thought: What if the charmed stone proves Mara is guilty of the accident that almost took her boyfriend's life?" Ron asked.

"But why steal the charmed stone now? She knew the police had it and that the investigation was closed. The auction wouldn't change anything, except that she could buy the stone back," Alice said.

"Guilt and fear can twist a person's logic. When she saw the charmed stone at A Witch's Thrift shop, that might have been enough to make her panic. Maybe she thought seeing it out of storage would be enough to prompt an officer to reopen the case and do an M-trace. I've seen people do stranger things out of fear."

"But then why did she say she was scared of a specific person?" Alice asked.

Ron frowned. "Mara may be scared that Ramsey or I am after her for a crime she really did commit. You have good intentions, but you may be covering for a criminal."

Alice thought about it, but it just didn't make sense. Mara had been running away from someone specific she called 'he,' and she said 'he' was dangerous. If the boyfriend was out of the country, it probably wasn't him, but that didn't rule out an officer at the station.

Someone here might have turned on her, and for all she knew, it was Ramsey, Ron, or any officer– Talented or Untalented. It all had to do with the car accident.

"If you had the charmed stone, you could tell if Mara was guilty or innocent, couldn't you?" Alice asked.

"Yes, but, Alice, you need to tell us where you saw her. If she's guilty, we need to bring her to justice, and if she's innocent and in trouble, I can't protect her while she's on the run."

Alice remained silent and still. In her gut, she did trust Ron. He was no villain. But could Alice trust him to make the right decisions on this? He seemed to want Mara to be a criminal, even though he allowed for the possibility that he was wrong.

Whatever she may have done in the past, Mara was well-liked now. It didn't seem likely she could kill someone. And if there really was someone from the police station that she thought was dangerous, could Alice take the chance of revealing her location even to Ron?

After a few minutes, Ron said, "If you hear it straight from Ramsey that no one here is out to hurt Mara, will you tell us where she is?"

Alice hesitated. "She's probably long gone," she said.

"Any information you can tell us can help," Ron said.

Alice nodded. "I'll tell you after I hear more from Ramsey."

Ron took the deal. He walked Alice straight through the police station to a group of desks in the back.

Ramsey was filling in paperwork and looked up when Ron approached. Ron started the conversation with an accusation.

"Ramsey, did you forget that you had a young lady waiting to speak with you?"

Ramsey blinked. "Um…no…I've just been swamped with that vandal case."

Alice caught of glimpse of Ramsey's screen before he clicked the window closed. He had it open to a picture of a storefront featuring a row of spray paint cans. They bore the same label as the one Alice had picked up outside of Many Treasures: Slick & Sleek Spray Paint. There were signs on the shelves that listed the price and the store name, but it was too blurry to read.

The window closed. Ramsey's home screen was a picture of him, an older woman, and a twenty-something man, probably his younger brother, on the day of Ramsey's graduation from the police academy. It was an endearing picture, if not for the wand in Ramsey's hand.

Alice looked around. Ramsey's desk was not in a cubicle like Ron's. They were out in the open for all to see and hear. Did the confusion spell work on desktop screens, too?

Ron noticed Alice looking around. In an abundance of caution, Ron said, "Put a silence spell around your desk."

Ramsey's eyebrows furled, but he took his wand out of his desk and tapped the metal surface three times. "What's wrong, Sarge?" he asked as he put his wand away.

"Do you remember a case three years ago involving Mara Blest's boyfriend?" Ron asked.

Ramsey shifted uncomfortably in his chair. A sign of guilt? Alice couldn't be sure.

"The Hawkson case. Yes, sir. I performed an M-trace on the vehicle," Ramsey said.

"There was a car charm. Did you perform an M-trace on that, too?" Ron asked.

Ramsey looked between Alice and Ron. "Why would I? It was a typical good luck charm."

Either Ramsey was a good actor, or he hadn't been covering for Mara. He seemed genuine about the car charm, but something was making him uncomfortable. He shifted in his seat again.

"You know a charmed stone can hold any kind of a spell," Ron said.

"Yes…but there wasn't a need to test it. They found a defect in the car itself." Ramsey started typing into the computer. He turned the screen around. It had a picture of a masculine looking blonde man, with a split lip and bruises all over his face. Alice turned her head away from the screen.

"What was the issue?" Ramsey said.

"A blown gasket caused the engine to combust."

"Any sign of tampering?" Ron asked.

"Not that I found," Ramsey said. He changed screens. Alice looked again and saw a page clearly titled M-trace. She couldn't understand most of it, except for the word "negative" which appeared in several places.

"Pull up the Untalented vehicle report. Just because

it wasn't magic, doesn't mean it wasn't physical sabotage."

Ramsey clicked through several screens. After a few seconds, he ran a hand through his hair and shook his head. There was no such screen.

"If I believed in coincidences, this would make the top of the list," Ron said.

"But you don't," Ramsey said, he seemed dismayed about it.

"No, so the question is who in this station would delete a file?" Ron asked.

It seemed more and more like Mara was right. Someone at the station had been involved in her boyfriend's case, at least. Alice wasn't sure how the charmed stone fit in or whether Mara was guilty or innocent, but Ramsey was sweating. Alice saw Ron notice it, too.

Ron gave Ramsey an order to compile a list of Untalented officers who had worked the case. Then he walked Alice back to a private room in the station. He closed the door.

"I'm not saying I don't distrust any of my officers, but I'm going to handle the case myself."

"I understand," Alice said.

"I need all the pieces if I'm going to fit this puzzle together. I have a feeling the charmed stone is the center of this case. Do you have any idea where I can look?"

Alice finally relented. "At her apartment plaza in one of the greenhouses that is currently undergoing renovation. That's where I saw her, but I doubt she's still there."

"I'll go there myself personally. Don't worry about Mara. I'll make sure nothing happens to her," Ron said.

He opened the door. Alice left, feeling no more reassured than when she had entered the station. As she walked down Main Street, she caught a glimpse of Titania driving a red Mercedes convertible with the top down. Her shining long hair flew behind her as she drove. Alice walked quickly behind a bus stop directory sign and waited for the car to pass. She was in no mood for Titania's pleading for a promise to keep her secrets. It was just another in a long line of worries starting with the affair and ending with Mara running for her life.

SIXTEEN

Burning Passions

"I don't know what to do," Alice said.

Back in Many Treasures, she had little to occupy her thoughts. Few people were coming to Magic Row after the vandalism the previous day. Even Eric and Puck were out, hopefully checking out schools for Puck to attend.

Naveed transformed into his Jinn form while there were no customers.

Alice went on, "I know Ron's going to do everything he can to protect Mara, even if she's guilty of a crime. But what if Ramsey is hiding something? What if he goes after her?"

"You told Ron everything, not Ramsey, right?" Naveed asked.

"Right," Alice said.

"So, he'll take care of it. It's not your problem."

"It's not about whether this is my responsibility. It's about what I can do for my friends."

"Your friends who think you're a witch, which you're

not. If you want to see if they're your real friends, reveal your secret," Naveed said.

"Secrets. That's another thing. What do I do about Titania and Tom? If I tell Liza, she'll be devastated."

Naveed was no help. His outdated advice included stoning and a hex on Tom's and Titania's backsides. Alice couldn't even begin to explain how many ways that was wrong.

"Do me a favor: Don't ever apply for a 'Dear Abby' columnist job," Alice said as she closed up Many Treasures for the day.

"Who is Abby?" Naveed asked, still in human form until the last light flicked off, and Alice opened the front door. *He knew the most obscure television references of the 21st century, but had never heard of Dear Abby?* Alice guessed even all-powerful jinn men were still loathed to read advice columns written by women.

"Never mind," Alice said.

Naveed, as a cat-jinn, led Alice to Reading & Co., where Celeste was already waiting with a latte in hand. Liza had not been able to reschedule lunch, but now that Hazel was working at A Witch's Thrift Shop, Celeste could take things a little easier on a Sunday.

Alice ordered her chai tea latte and sat as if weights were attached to her ankles and wrists. There was at least one metaphorical weight attached to her chest. Celeste looked her once over and stopped drinking her latte.

"What has you down?"

"Trouble. Nothing but trouble," Alice said.

"Man troubles?" Celeste asked.

"Man and woman: Two people who should not be together, being together where they shouldn't be," Alice said.

Alice's barely intelligible sentence lost Naveed's interest in the conversation. He wandered into the fortune reading room. Alice watched him go, frowning as she stared at the door. Celeste followed her eyes.

"Liza and Ron?" Celeste whispered.

Alice shook her head. If it had been Liza and Ron, she would have been happy for them. Zade and Hazel might have wanted their father back, but given what she knew about Tom, Ron was already a better father figure. Still, the decision was Liza's.

"I hope Liza hasn't chosen wrong," Alice said.

"Is this about Tom?" Celeste asked.

Alice pursed her lips. Celeste was not a gossip. Alice could trust her, and there were few people around to overhear. Maybe she could just ask her some general advice.

"What if Liza was right about Tom having had an affair three years ago?" Alice asked.

"You saw Tom with someone else?" Celeste was leaning forward and whispering, but Alice shushed her anyway. She hadn't expected Celeste to jump to that conclusion so quickly. Celeste moved her chair closer and said, "You have to tell me who was with him. You already started."

Alice glanced at the featured book, with the picture of Titania beside it as an advertisement for her upcoming book signing. Celeste's eyes positively shined. She smiled.

"Oh, that's rich!" she said. Then, she snorted derisively, adding, "And Tom has the nerve to come back here and try to patch things up with Liza?" Celeste shook her head.

"He does want to get back together with Alice and the kids, doesn't he?" Alice asked.

"That's what she told me this morning. And she's considering it." Celeste said.

Alice sipped her chai tea. The cinnamon spice radiated warmth through Alice's body. She allowed herself to hope that all would be well. "From what I overhead, the affair ended three years ago. Does it even matter now if they're both ready to move on?"

"It's not over if Tom's still meeting his mistress, is it?" Celeste said.

Alice couldn't explain that their meeting was related to Mara. She didn't want to expose the blackmail or theft. It wasn't her place.

Instead, she said, "It wasn't like that. Titania was worried about being exposed. She practically begged me not to tell Baz."

"That *is* rich," Celeste repeated.

She sipped her latte like the milk had soured, but the look in her eyes said she was relishing the bitter taste. Alice knew Celeste would keep the gossip to herself, but she must still have found the scandal sweet. To know something so personal and devastating about the town's hottest couple, it was going to be hard for Celeste not to walk around with that twinkle in her eyes that said: *"I know something you don't know."* Most people enjoyed sharing secrets, Alice suspected Celeste favored keeping them.

Alice's attention turned to the news board. The engagement picture of Titania and Baz thumbtacked to the wall stuck out. The photo was worth a thousand words, and all of them were synonyms for disaster.

"Do you think they're right for each other?" Alice asked.

Over the lip of her cup, Celeste asked, "Tom and Liza?"

"Them and Baz and Titania."

"Who am I to say who belongs together? I can say that Baz and Titania are a match made between two powerful wizard families. Some would say they were made for each other— or at least that they deserve each other."

"Yes, but does he deserve to marry someone who might not be faithful?"

"I notice you're not asking if Titania deserves a second chance. Why should Tom get a do-over and not Titania?" Celeste asked.

"I'm not thinking about Tom, I'm thinking about Liza and Zade and Hazel. Liza deserves not to be alone, and Zade and Hazel need a father."

"They need not to have their hearts broken."

"So, you think I should tell Liza?"

Celeste drank her latte and took a long moment to think. After a while, she said, "I don't know. It's not the easiest decision. If Titania and Tom are determined to remain faithful from here on out—"

Alice put an arm on Celeste's shoulder. The bell

above the café door rang. Suddenly, Alice was aware that there was a man seated nearby, a worker wiping a table, and a group of customers entering the shop. At least Liza's Reading Room door was still closed.

"You can't tell anyone. I don't want Baz, Liza, the kids—anyone— to find out like that. It'll break their hearts to hear it through town gossip."

"My lips are sealed— with a spell if you'd like," Celeste said.

"Not necessary. I trust you."

"Then why do you still look so miserable?" Celeste asked.

Alice was clutching her cup like she was holding on for dear life. In this case, it was the love-lives of people who had become dear to her. She let go and sighed.

"Not telling seems wrong. But telling could have repercussions, too. Shouldn't I just butt out because none of this is my business?"

"We all know how well you keep out of other people's business."

"Ouch," Alice said. "Am I that nosey?"

Celeste patted her hand, "We'll just say unnaturally interested. But that's a good thing. You wouldn't know any of us on Magic Row if you weren't a curious one. But I think this has the potential to change a lot of lives in Urbana. Titania and Baz's relationship is not just about them. The Knights are influential in mage politics, and the Delvauxs own most of Urbana's magical properties. Their alliance would make Urbana one of the most powerful magical towns in America."

Alice pressed her lips tight together. Telling Liza

would affect the kids, telling Baz might affect all of Urbana. The information made the decision that much harder.

"If you ask me," a voice came from the table directly beside them. A man with white hair turned around. Rhys Merlin revealed himself to have been sitting there who knows how long, drinking a green tea, and doing a crossword.

Either the room had heated or Alice's cheeks had. She fought the urge to bury her head in her hands. It served her right for having a very private conversation in such a public place. There were a lot fewer people around after yesterday's attack on A Witch's Thrift Shop, but the fact that a powerful wizard like Rhys had overheard meant Alice had not been careful enough.

Rhys continued, "I'd say you tell a powerful person, anonymously, and let them handle it. This person would investigate the matter and draw a conclusion about what was best for the Knights and Delvauxs."

Celeste said, "I didn't think you did private investigator work, Rhys."

"I'm not talking about myself," he replied.

"You said 'a powerful person.' I thought you were the most powerful mage in Urbana?" Alice asked.

"Magically speaking, you're right. But power comes in many forms. And in ways that matter to Talented and Untalented people alike, I'm not the most powerful *person* in the community."

"Then who is?" Alice asked.

Celeste answered, "Oh no, Alice isn't going within a foot of Mr. Delvaux."

Alice said, "Baz? I'm not afraid of him. I just don't want to hurt him."

"You are not capable of hurting Baz, not on this matter. It was Baz's uncle who arranged his engagement with Titania. And what his uncle has put together, I suspect Baz wouldn't be hurt to have a cheating man put asunder," Rhys said.

"But even if it's true," Celeste said, "Perseus Delvaux will not believe you. He never believes anything but what he sees with his own eyes. When his mind is made up, not even his nephew's opinions matter much to him."

Rhys nodded, "He'll investigate. He wouldn't risk a bad union ruining the family name. Besides, I think he wouldn't mind the news coming from you, Alice."

Alice didn't want to decode Rhys' meaning on that one. She was sure it had to do with her last name being Adelcraft, alluding to an ancient magical heritage. Only Celeste and Naveed knew that Alice had inherited zero magical ability.

"I advise against this," Celeste said in a high-pitched voice, shaking her head before finishing off her latte.

Rhys stood, swung his coat on, and took the last word, "And I can only advise Alice to follow her heart." He winked and walked out the door.

Alice bit her lip. She really didn't know what her heart was telling her. She pushed her chai tea away. The cinnamon spice was burning her throat.

She nearly choked when Baz entered the shop. He strolled up to the counter and put in his order. Alice could not take her eyes off of him as he made a minimal amount of small talk with the cashier.

"You like him, don't you?" Celeste whispered.

"What? No," Alice said.

"It would explain why you're taking this so personally."

"I'm not taking it personally at all; I just want to make the right decision."

Alice's tone was hushed, but Celeste answered much louder than was necessary when she repeated Rhys' advice in a singsong voice, "Follow your heart."

"Follow your heart on what?" Liza said, coming out of the Fortune Room and nodding good-bye to her last customer. She had Naveed in her arms and set him down on an empty chair before dragging one over for herself.

"Alice is denying that she has feelings for a man because she can't possibly believe he'd feel the same way about her." Celeste grinned. Alice put her attention on her chai tea latte and pursed her lips.

Liza nodded. "It's Baz, isn't it?"

The cup slipped from Alice's fingers. She scrambled to grab the napkins at the center of the table and sop up the spill. Celeste waved a hand and dried the table using magic, which only caused Alice to redden.

Liza apologized, adding, "I didn't mean to be so blunt."

"What makes you think that I *like Baz*?" Alice whispered

Liza shrugged, "I don't know. The way you look at him and he at you. I noticed it yesterday."

"I don't remember ever making googly eyes at him." Alice's tone made it sound like she had something to defend.

Celeste snickered, "You're not the googly-eye type. It's more an attempt to smother a rising flame of passion."

Liza said, "There's an unspoken awareness of each other. You move around him. Your eyes avoid his, but when they lock, they aren't easily separated."

"Gives me chills," Celeste said.

"You're reading too much into it." Alice tried taking a nonchalant sip of her tea and looking away.

Celeste would not relent. "There's definitely something under the surface."

"Well, it's not going to happen. For more than one reason," Alice eyed Celeste. What she was not saying, besides the engagement and Titania's affair, was that Alice was not a witch. And Baz was just the kind of wizard to whom things like that mattered.

"You never know. Fate has a way of making things happen," Liza said.

"Like right now." Celeste glanced up, and Alice followed her eyes to the counter.

Baz had a white paper bag in his hand and was walking not to the door, but over to Alice, Liza, and Celeste.

He bowed his head and said simply, "Ladies."

"Good afternoon, Baz," Celeste said.

Baz smiled curtly. "Celeste, Liza, I'm sure you've received the invitations for this Saturday's engagement celebration."

"We have," Celeste said.

Liza nodded.

Baz turned to Alice. Again, his ice-blue eyes sent chills down Alice's spine. She tensed in an attempt to keep control. "Miss Adelcraft, it is customary for my family to invite all members of Magic Row to such a large event. I realize Many Treasures is not one of my buildings. Still, I would be delighted if you and the Kinjo family would attend the evening's festivities."

Much like a magician, he seemed to pull two white envelopes out of thin air. Gold embroidered letters formally addressed *Miss Alice Adelcraft* and *Mrs. Rin Kinjo & Family*. Alice tried not to blush as she took the cards.

"Thank you and, uh, congratulations," Alice said.

Baz hesitated. Alice could understand now what Liza meant when she said they were difficult to separate when their eyes met. The flame Celeste had mentioned rose into Alice's chest. She went hot and cold all over, with a burning in her chest and an icy tingling on her skin.

Alice had never felt this way in her life. And then it was over. Baz bowed his head, wished the ladies a good day, and walked out of Alice's sights.

Celeste and Liza shared annoyingly smug smiles. Naveed jumped off the table and stretched as if he couldn't take another moment of sitting around talking. He was ready for the lunch that Alice had promised to pick up before her afternoon shift at Many Treasures.

Alice thanked Liza and Celeste for the company. Then she and Naveed left Reading & Co. They headed over to the Chinese restaurant near Merlin's Shadow.

Alice would have thought Naveed would be as hungry as a lion, but when they reached the restaurant, he walked right past it.

"Hey!" Alice called out, but Naveed had disappeared.

Alice took five quick steps past the restaurant. The alley there disappeared, and Alice was standing in front of Merlin's Shadow. The place was surrounded with witch and wizard spectators, police tape, and officers. Alice stopped one and asked, "What happened? Did the vandal attack again?"

"No, miss, now please step back," said an officer.

He waved Alice into the crowd. An old lady standing next to Alice, whom she recognized as one of yesterday's customers in Many Treasures, heard the question and answered, "This is much more frightening than a vandal. There was a fire!"

SEVENTEEN

A Shadow in Flames

Yellow tape floated around the entrance as a magical barrier to the building. Alice tried moving around the tape, but each time she reached over, or under the barrier, the tape rose up to smack her hand. It hit hard, too, like a rubber band snapping. Alice rubbed her skin and frowned.

She could at least walk around to where she could see the building entrance. So far, just two officers cordoned off the area with the yellow tape. They kept the residents back. When she saw officer Ramsey come out of the place, Alice gasped.

A million thoughts ran through her brain, like: *Had Ramsey chased Mara down here and attacked her? Or had Mara set the fire in the process of escaping?* The crowd around the building at first seemed to suggest it was the vandal.

"I tell you, this is an escalation of what's been happening all over town," one man said.

A woman holding a baby added, "It's the old witch hunters. They're after mages!"

"It's a rogue girl, probably jealous of the Talented, who's running around with a charmed stone causing trouble."

Alice turned her head sharply to see who had made the last comment. It was an older gentleman in a check-ered blue and green sweater and faded navy blue dress pants. He looked like he could be any of Alice's neigh-bors, though most of Alice's neighbors kept to them-selves. This man seemed willing to talk.

Alice slid between bystanders, making her way over to him. Once she was two steps away, she asked. "Excuse me, did you say it was a woman?"

"Yes, a pretty young girl with purple hair."

Alice felt a tingling in her spine. That was Mara. But she wasn't the vandal unless her hair could turn a reddish-brown at will.

"How do you know she was the vandal who set the fire?"

"I saw her with my own two eyes, running away. An officer was chasing after her," the man said.

"I saw the same thing in my crystal ball," a teen girl with bright-shining braces added.

Several people confirmed the sighting of the officer and the girl running away. Alice had a horri-fying moment in which she wondered whether she had tipped off the officer that Mara had feared. If so, it wasn't Ramsey. And if Alice had gotten Mara into this mess, she had to do something to get her out of it.

"In what direction did she go?" Alice asked.

At the very same moment, the officer nearest Alice

picked something up on his radio. He unlatched the radio and spoke into it, "Please repeat that."

Between radio static, the words came in clear. "Officer down, Main, and Third street."

Alice looked down at her feet. Naveed had curled around her leg and was now looking up at her. She bent down and scooped him into her arms.

Ramsey grabbed the radio. "What's the officer's name and status?"

An excruciating few seconds of radio static "Unidentifiable."

Ramsey clicked on the radio again, "What is the name on the uniform?"

Static. "Sir, the officers at the scene are saying it's Ramsey. With whom am I speaking? Is that you, Quinton?"

Ramsey clicked off the radio and held it away from himself. He turned beat-red, took out a handkerchief, and dabbed his forehead. Clicking the talk button again, he said, "Yeah, this is Ramsey. The other man is an imposter."

"I'll relay that to the two men on scene."

"What's the status of the man?" Ramsey said.

"Unclear, the officers are not responding to my inquiry. Give me a minute."

Ron waited a few seconds, looking miserable. He could not a full minute before clicking the talk button again. "What's the status of the suspect who supposedly injured the man?"

The dispatcher on the radio said, "Female suspect was last seen running down Main toward Fourth street."

Into the radio, Ramsey said, "Your suspect is Mara Blest, B-L-E-S-T."

"Got it here. Sir, I'm getting static interference from the officers on scene. I'll send out more officers."

"No need. I'm in direct pursuit."

"Sir?"

"That's an order," Ramsey said.

"Copy that," came the response.

Ramsey handed the radio back to the officer and issued his last order. "Rhys has the fire contained and is doing repairs. Wait for his order, then let everyone back into the building."

"Yes, sir," the officer said.

"Ramsey," Alice called out. "You need to take me with you. Maybe I can talk Mara down."

Ramsey turned to Alice, "I'm sorry, but I'm going to have to ask you to stay here. I can't let a civilian get involved in any crossfire."

"I don't think Mara would kill anyone."

"She may have killed someone today. I'm sorry, Alice. I know you like to think the best of people, but people aren't always what they seem."

A spectator cleared his throat. It was the man in his checkered sweater and glasses. He pushed his frames up on his nose and stared at Ramsey in concern. "Sorry to interrupt, but I heard the officer down was Ramsey. Is it your brother?"

Ramsey tensed. He forced a smile. "No, Mr. Ohn, Dar's not an officer, but thanks for your concern," Ramsey said, then he walked in the opposite direction, waving the yellow tape away with his wand and leaving the scene.

"Mr. Ohn?" Alice asked. Her curiosity had peaked.

"Yes?" Mr. Ohn held his glasses frame as he looked down at Alice.

"You said Ramsey had a brother?" Alice pictured the younger man next to Ramsey on his desktop background. The man had *brownish-red hair.*

"Yes, a younger one: Darwyn. Poor boy." Mr. Ohn leaned forward, whispering, "He's Untalented."

This struck Alice as curious. She couldn't see how it was connected as yet, but she was sure he was connected somehow with the events in Magic Row lately. She had to find out more.

"Why did you assume he was an officer?" Alice asked.

"He joined the academy three years ago. The academy is for everyone, mind you, except there are a few extra courses for Talented officers."

Ramsey had an Untalented younger brother who had joined the academy three years ago? That was the same time as Mara's boyfriend. Ron said he hadn't seen a connection between Quinton Ramsey and Mara Blest before her boyfriend's car accident, but there was one. Darwyn Ramsey and Vaughn Hawkson had been in the police academy together.

Urbana was not so large a city that two cadets would not know each other. Had they been friends? Enemies? Hawkson was Talented, and Darwyn was Untalented, that right there had the makings of a rivalry. Had

Darwyn been the "officer" who had helped Mara and turned on her now?

There was only one way to find out. Disregarding Ramsey's orders, Alice whispered to Naveed, "Take me to Third Street and Main." Naveed looked toward Third and concentrated.

Alice was getting used to the rushing sensation of magical travel. The key was not holding her breath. The jolt to the system each time knocked the air out of her, so she let go this time and breathed normally. She still felt a little winded, but there was no nausea now.

The sight on the sidewalk, however, made her feel plenty sick without the element of magical travel. Instead of one officer down, there were two lying flat on their backs. One had a hole in the chest of his uniform and a good-sized burn by his heart. Naveed looked around and saw the street had been cleared, probably by the officers before Alice and Naveed had arrived. Naveed transformed out of his cat form and checked for a pulse.

"There's a heartbeat." Naveed pealed the cloth off of the man's skin. "There's something strange about the wound. It's getting worse by the second," Naveed said.

The other officer stirred. He brought a hand to the back of his head and moaned. Alice went to him and knelt down. She helped to lift him to a seated position. He grunted and clutched his side.

"Easy. What happened?" Alice asked.

"We thought a cadet was down, but it wasn't an officer. It was the vandal. He had a charmed stone. I've never seen anything like it." The man coughed and held his side tighter. He was breathing heavily and sweating as he spoke. Each word was laborious and the officer stopped now and then, wincing in pain. "I think it might be infused with a magic stealing spell. He used my own magic against me."

Alice turned to Naveed, "Can you heal them?"

Naveed shook his head. "I don't know this magic. They need a mage physician and soon."

"Take them to the hospital." Alice stood up. She thought she saw a man across the street in a hoodie. His brown hair was shining red in the sunlight.

"What about you?" Naveed asked.

"I'll be fine." Alice said.

Naveed practically growled. "You can't go after this man alone. Look what he did to these people."

"Then I wish you'd hurry back," Alice said.

She meant it. She didn't want to go after a magic-stealing vandal, but she didn't have any magic for him to steal. This was the one case in which Alice hoped being Untalented might actually work in her favor. She only wished she could stop the vandal, or Darwyn Ramsey as she could probably call him, from harming Mara Blest.

EIGHTEEN

Kidnapped

A lice had lost track of Darwyn by the time she had crossed the street. A few buildings down a familiar storefront came into view. It was a garage on one side with plenty of space for fixing up vehicles. The other side was a small shop with car-care items.

Alice had never owned a car, but she had seen the shop before. Most recently, she remembered the row of shelves with Slick & Sleek Spray Paint cans from seeing it on Ramsey's computer screen. This was the shop where the vandal–Darwyn– had gotten his paint cans.

A woman outside was smoking and pacing back and forth. She looked sideways at Alice and stopped, but her hand was shaking. She was definitely nervous.

"We're closed," the woman said when Alice approached.

"In the middle of the day?" Alice asked. The woman did not respond. Alice continued, "Did an officer come in here?" Alice asked.

Alice heard a scream coming from inside. The

woman threw her cigarette to the floor and stepped on it. "That's it. I'm out. If he thinks I'm doing this for him, he's crazy."

"Who? Darwyn? Does he work here?" Alice asked.

"Look, he's a good kid, I guess, but he's gone crazy. First that girl comes in here then he's chasing after her— in a police outfit! —and he says *she's* unstable. Then another cop goes inside and orders me out here. I don't even know if he's a real cop. I got no one on the floor. Everybody's out to lunch. What am I supposed to do, argue with two deranged guys?"

"You could call the police. Ask for Ron Knight," Alice said.

"No way. You do it. I'm out," she spun on her heels and started walking toward the nearest bus stop. Under her breath, she was mumbling, "I don't get paid for this..." or something similar.

Alice wanted to wait for Naveed, but this was her chance. She walked inside the store. The lights were off, except for the rays streaming in from the garage workshop. The windows facing the workshop floor were up high up, so Alice had to raise herself up to get a better view.

She could hear voices coming from inside the garage. The most prominent one was Officer Ramsey. He was telling Darwyn to put something down, but Alice couldn't tell what without looking.

Spotting an empty wood crate among a pile of boxes, Alice grabbed it. She flipped it over and slid it under the window. Alice stepped on. She stood slowly, bringing herself just high enough to see into the garage.

Darwyn had the rock– no, Mara's charmed stone!– in one hand. He had it pointed toward Mara while Ramsey stood between them with his hands up. Ramsey took a step toward Darwyn, but Darwyn only held the stone up higher.

"Don't do this. Let this end now," Ramsey said.

"No! You don't get to tell me what to do. I have the power here."

"You have one power, one limited power, Dar."

"Limited? Limited is the entrance stone you gave me. What was I supposed to do with that? This one, this one has real power."

"It's charmed to drain magic. It'll only harm you if you try to use it," Ramsey said.

Darwyn's eyes were nearly bulging from his head. "Did you forget I grew up among mages just like you? I know how to reverse a charmed stone. It doesn't even take magic to do it. It's just a matter of engraving the right words, and we have plenty of tools around here to do that."

"You make it steal energy from others," Ramsey said, putting it together.

Darwyn laughed with a hint of hysteria. "Got a little power already: Two mages officers. I don't want to have to take your magic, Quint, but I will if I have to."

"I'm not stepping aside," Ramsey said.

"Darwyn, please don't do this," Mara pleaded through tears.

"No, *you* don't do this! You don't get to keep playing me for a fool. You're not as innocent as you want everyone else to think. None of this would have happened if it wasn't for you. It was all for you!"

The light went on in the shop. Alice ducked, hoping no one had seen her. She heard a shot that sounded like lightning, Ramsey shouting, "No!," and a scrummage coming from within the garage. Then there was silence —all except the clicking of heels.

"Hello?" A voice called out.

Titania Knight appeared between the shelves. Alice jumped off the crate and walked up to her. Titania smiled smugly, saying, "You work here, too? I guess Many Treasures doesn't pay so well."

"Titania," Alice said between gritted teeth.

"I'm sorry," Titania said. "Have you decided if you're going to do the right thing?"

"What?" Alice asked.

"Are you going to keep my secret?" Titania asked.

"Now is not the time," Alice said, glancing at the door to the garage and hoping Darwyn wouldn't storm through it any minute.

"Look, I don't know what level mage you are, but Baz has a suspicion you are not a level nine. I may not have a lot of magic, but I know a lot of powerful people."

"Are you threatening me?" Alice asked.

Titania ignored her. "Of course not. I'm just here to pick my red Mercedes from its tune-up. Did you know it was a birthday gift from Baz?" Titania said. She smiled and pushed past Alice.

"No, Titania, don't go in there!" Alice warned.

It was too late. Titania walked too far in not to be

seen. Alice had no choice but to duck back by the window and continue watching the scene unfold.

"What is going on here?" Titania said.

Alice raised herself up to look through the window again. Mara was down on the floor. Ramsey had his wand out and pointed toward Darwyn. An Untalented should have been scared with a wizard pointing a wand in his direction, but Darwyn was laughing.

"Looks like I get to take the magic of a Knight. Too bad it's the weakest one." Darwyn raised the charmed stone.

"Don't take your wand out," Ramsey told Titania, "He'll use your own magic against you."

Titania said, "He's Untalented. How can he use any magic against me?"

"I don't need your magic," Darwyn said. "I just took Mara's."

"No!" Ramsey placed himself between Darwyn and Titania.

"You know you're not going to stop me, Quint. Quit trying," Darwyn said.

Ramsey lifted his wand, pointing it to a stack of tires behind Darwyn. "I'm sorry," he said.

Before he could hit the tires, Darwyn aimed the charmed stone at him. A beam of blue light shot out. Ramsey was hit. He flew back, hit the wall, and rolled until he fell unconscious on the floor.

Titania screamed. Darwyn pointed the stone at her, but this time he was shaking. "He made me do it!" Darwyn shouted. His face was red, and his eyes were tearing.

"I'm not involved in this. I shouldn't be here!" Titania said.

"Shut up," Darwyn said. His face grew red.

Darwyn raised his palms to Titania's neck. Alice's first thought was that he might rush forward and strangle her. But Darwyn's charmed stone blazed. Titania began to scream—then stopped abruptly.

Touching her throat, Titania tried to make a sound. Nothing came out. Darwyn had done the impossible: he had silenced Titania Knight.

Titania turned away from Darwyn in a last ditch effort to run away. He lifted the stone again. This time, Titania froze. Since she was facing the shop, Alice could see her mouthing something unladylike before bursting into tears.

Darwyn chuckled. His laughter was unhinged, too loud, and shaky for a stable man. "Cat got your tongue? I always wished I could do that…me and half the town I'm sure," Darwyn said. Then he turned, and whatever amusement had been on his face was gone.

His eyes were watery and bloodshot, his face sweaty and reddening with rage. He looked like a man who could kill – a man who might have just killed his own brother. He turned his eyes to Mara, his prey, who lay unconscious on the ground. He knelt down and moved a strand of hair away from Mara's face.

"It didn't have to be this way," Darwyn said.

Alice wanted to cry out, to stop him, anything! But what could she do? She did not have the magic to defend herself against a wizard.

Alice whispered, "Naveed, where are you?"

The crate on which Alice was standing, creaked. Alice barely had time to say, *"Uh-Oh,"* before the wood snapped. She crashed to the floor, not in the office, but in the garage with Darwyn staring over her.

"You," Darwyn said. "What were you doing eaves-dropping like that?"

Titania made a whimpering sound, but she still couldn't move. The hex on her held strong enough to keep her trapped in place. Darwyn walked toward Alice, and she scooted away from him.

"I'm not going to hurt you. I'm just going to take your magic." Darwyn kept a firm grasp on the stone.

Alice stood and dusted herself off. She couldn't defend herself, but all was not lost. Assuming Naveed would not let her down, she could still save herself and the others. All she had to do was stall.

"Why now, Darwyn? Why not steal the stone three years ago when you first helped Mara plant it in her boyfriend's car?" Alice asked.

Darwyn smiled. "I'm sure I don't know what you mean."

Alice took another step back, closer to Titania and the door. "You grew up in the mage community. Your brother had powers, but you don't. Your friends had powers, friends like Mara. You grew up with her, right? Let me guess. She was nice, fun to be with, someone you could see yourself with as more than a friend. She wouldn't be with you, though, would she? She chose another mage, a handsome, foreign wizard entering the police academy: Vaughn Hawkson."

"He wasn't worthy of the badge," Darwyn said.

"That's right. Hawkson was abusive. He hurt Mara, and you were determined to protect her. Was the charmed stone your idea?"

"She had to make one, to drain his power. He was a madman."

"A madman, yes," Alice said. She found the word ironic coming from Darwyn. At the moment, he couldn't have looked more insane.

He ran a shaky hand through his hair. "She felt guilty for using it. Guilty! Can you imagine? She told me she wished she'd never put it in his car."

"That's because she thought it was responsible for the accident."

"No, no. She knew it was the car itself."

"Yes, that's right," Alice said. She thought through the police report. The police would have told Mara that the car had malfunctioned. But the shop that evaluated the car…that page had been missing. Alice realized why. "It was a malfunction, but not an accident, right? Your brother discovered it was your shop that had last worked on the car; he covered that up. He covered for Mara, too, by not testing the charmed stone. Or maybe he hadn't even thought about it. It couldn't affect the car after all, but Mara thought it had played a role in the accident."

"The charm drained his powers. That's all it did."

Alice thought back to Ron's comment about a mage protecting himself. She figured out why Mara thought the charmed stone had contributed to his death. "He might have been able to protect himself if he had his powers, so by using the charmed stone she had weakened him enough for the accident to cause real damage," Alice said.

Mara moaned and twitched on the floor. Darwyn aimed the stone at her. Alice had to keep him distracted.

She kept talking. "Why…why did Mara run? That's the one thing I don't understand. She knew the police had the charmed stone. Why did the auction freak her out?"

Darwyn broke his stare at Mara. He looked at Alice. "She forgot me. I never forgot her. This was my chance to make her remember…remember what I did for her."

"You told her what you did to the car," Alice realized. That was why she said he was dangerous. And why she didn't go to the police. She had no way of knowing what lengths the elder Ramsey would go to protect his brother, Darwyn.

Darwyn aimed the stone at Mara again.

"You love her," Alice said.

Darwyn gripped the stone tighter. His knuckles were almost white. "No, I hate her. I hate all of you. Thinking you're better than the rest of us. But look at what I can do with one stone."

The stone glowed.

"Is that why you vandalized anything important to the mage community? Is it why you set fire to Merlin's Shadow?"

"I had to get this stone. And now that I have it—"

"Now that you have it, you used it to hurt your brother."

Darwyn closed his eyes and shook his head. "I told him to stop."

"Yes," Alice said softly. "But he didn't attack you because he loves you. You can say you hate all mages, but you don't. You love your brother, and you care for Mara. You're still bound to this community through them. Don't hurt the people you love."

Darwyn wiped his eyes with the sleeve of his cadet uniform, the stone shook in his hand. He looked like he might relent, dropping the stone. But then he turned to Alice and screamed, "Stop! Stop talking, *witch*!"

Darwyn ran forward, his arm struck Alice's face. She braced herself for the fall but landed hard. Alice cried out in fear and pain. She rolled onto her back and stared up at Darwyn's contorted face. He readied another blow.

Where was Naveed? Without his magic, there was no way for Alice to defend herself.

Alice put her hands up instinctively, her palms facing outward. Darwyn flinched, his hand reached for the stone and fumbled as the chain-linked with a button. He was nervous, thinking she was going to use her powers against him.

This was her chance!

Alice grabbed for the necklace. Darwyn pulled back. For a minute, they were locked in a high-stakes game of tug and war. The chain snapped, and the charmed stone rolled across the floor.

"No!" Darwyn lunged for it, but just as he was about to reach it, it shot across the floor. It hit the tower of tires and stopped. Darwyn was still closer to it than Alice, but it was far enough that Mara had the upper hand.

"Catching a witch off guard—not cool Darwyn," Mara said. She had her wand pointed firmly toward Darwyn.

"Mara," Darwyn's voice became small and shaky. "You and I are equal now. I did this all for you."

"You tried to steal my magic. You almost killed me." Mara kept her wand straight and steady. Somewhere inside herself, she had found her courage.

"No, you're wrong. I didn't try to steal your magic," Darwyn said softly. His teary-eyed expression changed to a malice-filled grin. "I did steal it," he said, lunging for the stone.

"Not all of it," Mara replied.

Mara sent a shot from her wand, which hit Darwyn in the shoulder. He fell, and smoke rose from his singed sleeve. He clamored on the ground, still searching for the stone.

"No, no, where is it?" Darwyn cried out.

Alice felt something on her foot and heard a soft "meow." She looked down. There was Naveed with the charmed stone in his mouth. Slowly, she bent down to retrieve the stone without anyone noticing.

"What's going on?" Ramsey stirred and sat up. Mara went to help him.

"You're alive?" Darwyn stood up. "I didn't mean to hurt you," he said. Tears streamed down his cheeks.

Ramsey replied, "I know. Darwyn, you need to stop this." With Mara's help, Ramsey got to his feet. He took a step forward, saying with gentle persuasion, "Give up this fight."

"I can't," Darwyn said, crying.

The door burst open, first the entrance to the side-shop, then the garage doors opened wide. Darwyn lifted his hand to shield his eyes from the array of flashlights. Ron lead a team of four officers into the shop. All had their wands out and aimed.

Baz came in through the side door. With a wave of his wand, he undid the spell on Titania. She launched into a barrage of angry exclamations and tears. Baz did little to comfort her. Instead, he said to Ron, "Get the stone."

Ron pulled Darwyn to his feet. Darwyn tried to run, but Ron had a firm grip on his wrist. He snapped the cuff around one wrist. Then, as Darwyn swung at him, Ron caught his other wrist, twisted him around and snapped the cuffs around it. "He doesn't have it," Ron said.

Alice was about to reveal that she had the stone when Ramsey slammed into Ron. The unexpected blow forced Ron to the ground. Ramsey pointed his wand at Darwyn, and the cuffs opened.

"Run!" Ramsey said.

Mara shrieked, "How could you defend him?"

Darwyn ran for the red convertible, causing Titania to scream. Baz pointed his wand at the car tires, and they deflated in seconds. The officers surrounded Darwyn so that there was no escape.

Baz turned his attention to Ron and Ramsey's struggle. Ramsey had just struck Ron's jaw. Ron stumbled back. Baz pointed his wand at the cuffs on the floor, so the next time Ramsey swung, the metal caught his wrist.

Ramsey pulled his arm back, tugging against the cuffs. Ron took the opportunity to land a blow in Ramsey's face. Ramsey fell against the concrete. He was out cold. The cuffs found his other hand and clicked shut. Once they were secured, the metal cuffs glowed orange and then faded back to silver. It was a magical seal to ensure they could not be spelled off.

"Next time seal it magically—even if it's an Untalented," Baz said.

"Will do," said Ron.

Titania ran forward, right past Baz to her car.

"Oh my poor baby," Titania said, gently caressing the hood.

"Titania, get back!" Baz shouted.

Darwyn had not been handcuffed yet. He grabbed Titania and wrapped his hand around her neck. The officers aimed their wands, but Ron ordered them not to fire. Darwyn used Titania to shield himself. The officers backed off, all except Ron, whom Darwyn was moving toward.

"I will snap her neck. I mean it!" Darwyn said.

Ron stepped back. Darwyn advanced, keeping his back to the tires. Ron and Baz had no choice but to move to the side, opening a path between Darwyn and the shop door. Darwyn stopped at the tires and nodded to Alice. She was the only thing now standing between Darwyn and his exit.

"You too, move," Darwyn said.

Alice looked down at Naveed, moving her chin forward and eyeing the tower of tires. She couldn't make a wish aloud, but she hoped Naveed understood what she wanted. He walked behind her ankles, then Alice could no longer feel his fur.

"Go on, move!" Darwyn was losing his patience. He tightened his old on Titania's neck and she sobbed. Her eyes pleaded with Alice.

Alice raised her hands. The charmed stone hung through her fingers for everyone to see. It was not just clearly visible; it was glowing such a bright blue it almost looked purple. She hadn't intended to use it, but it was doing something. Darwyn's eyes widened.

"Give that to me," Darwyn said.

"Let go of Titania, and we'll trade," Alice said.

"You think I'm stupid? If I let go of her, they'll attack me," Darwyn said.

"I'm giving you a chance. I could just attack you right now," Alice said.

"Nice try, but you don't have a wand, and the charmed stone doesn't work on an Untalented. All the rest of you with wands, if you try anything, Titania is dead."

"I don't need a wand," Alice said.

She spied Naveed on the topmost tire and nodded. The tires began to fall. Darwyn turned and attempted to protect himself as the tower enveloped him. Titania pulled away from his grasp and ran into Baz's arms.

Ron and the officers took the tires off of the unconscious Untalented. Baz awkwardly patted Titania's shoulders and pulled her off of him. He walked to Alice.

"I'll take the charmed stone," he said.

Alice handed it to him. "Are you going to perform an M-trace on it?"

"Yes." Baz looked at the stone curiously. While it had glowed brightly in Alice's hand, it dimmed when Baz took it into his grip.

"What happens to Mara?" Alice asked, watching as Ron also took her into custody.

Baz placed the stone in an evidence bag and floated it to Ron. "If the M-trace reveals her magic as the one on the stone, she may be charged with unlawful use of her powers. I doubt she'll be charged for her boyfriend's attempted murder, given that Darwyn was responsible for the sabotage."

"You know about that?" Alice asked.

"Ron followed your tip and investigated The Green Houses. He called me in to do the M-trace, as I have the magic necessary to identify the person who cast a spell on an object. We didn't find the stone, but we did find a threatening note from Mara's boyfriend reading 'I know what you did.' It's likely what scared Mara into running in the first place," said Baz.

"I don't understand. Didn't Ron say the boyfriend was still in his home country?"

"He is. Which is why we performed an M-trace on the note," Baz said.

"What did you find?" Alice was genuinely intrigued.

"The same residual magic as was on the stone in A Witch's Thrift Shop. What I was detecting was magic in a simple charmed stone that allowed entrance and exit to magical places around Urbana," Baz said.

"The amber stone. When I first saw the vandal, uh, Darwyn, I mean, he was wearing an amber-colored charmed stone," Alice said.

"That must be the one. It contained magic that infuses itself on the wearer and whatever he touches while he is using it," Baz said.

"So, Darwyn wrote the note. Your M-trace revealed that he used the magic on the charmed stone to get it to Mara in Magic Row." Alice nodded. It was all making sense.

Baz continued, "The M-trace also revealed, to a skilled wizard, that the magic was that of the Ramsey family."

"Quint Ramsey. He made the entrance stone for his brother," Alice said.

"That was my conclusion. That and the report of the injured officers a block from here made it easy to trace Darwyn here, to his workplace," Baz said.

"And you came just in time," said Titania, who had been eavesdropping. She walked up to Baz and wrapped her slender arms around his broad shoulders. He seemed to stiffen as Titania pressed her cheek to his. "Oh, Baz, you saved my life," Titania said.

Technically, Naveed had saved her, but Alice wasn't going to point out that she had a cat-jinn on her side. Alice felt queasy again, probably the shock and adrenaline catching up to her. Titania's deflected attempt to kiss Baz may have also had something to do with it. Was it Alice's imagination, or were his eyes refusing to let Alice go, despite all of Titania's advances?

No. It wasn't that. Baz was just not one for public displays of affection, and Titania was embarrassing him.

He gently pushed Titania back, whispering, "Please, not here. You must restrain yourself."

Alice looked away from the couple. She spotted Naveed walking away from the tires. He headed toward the garage door, where, curiously, Hex was sitting with her tail curled around her. Had she watched the whole scene without getting involved? Alice had no idea, actually, what the female jinn was feeling—Alice was new to interpreting expressions on a cat.

Naveed walked toward Hex, but the moment it was clear he was trying to reach her, she got up and ran away. Naveed stopped and stared at the empty space where she'd been.

"I'd better be going," Alice excused herself from Baz and Titania. Naveed saw her walking out of the garage. Alice gave him a sympathetic smile and bent her head, gesturing for him to follow. Together, but alone in their thoughts, the two walked silently side by side, all the way home.

NINETEEN

The Charmed Stone

A lice was too exhausted that night to do anything but sleep. The Kinjos gave her the next day off to prepare for her interview at the museum. Alice had utterly forgotten about it. She had previously prepared for it, practicing her answers for the various questions. But she needed a refresher. Alice paced around her apartment, trying to concentrate, but she found her thoughts returning again and again to Magic Row.

"What's there to worry about? Everything worked out fine," Naveed said.

"You're right. Darwyn is in custody. Mara would likely get a light sentence. No one was killed in the fire. I should be happy," Alice said.

"You forgot the most important one: No one discovered your secret," Naveed said.

"I'm not sure anymore that I am Untalented."

Naveed raised an eyebrow.

"The charmed stone glowed more in my hands than anyone's. Why?" Alice said.

Naveed shrugged. "It doesn't mean you're Talented."

"No, but it has to mean something." Alice sat beside Naveed on the couch. "In Mrs. Kinjo's photo album, there's a picture of me as a teen where I'm wearing a charmed stone. Why would I have a charmed stone?" Alice asked.

Naveed rolled his eyes. "It's no mystery. Your father was a wizard. He probably gave you a stone infused with a good luck spell. Human parents give those kinds of things to their children."

"Yes, but I remember it being a gift from my mother. She wasn't Talented."

"Perhaps your father gave it to her, and she passed it to you," Naveed said.

"Maybe…" Alice said.

She stood and paced around the living room. On her tenth time pacing, she bumped into Naveed. Alice hadn't seen him get up, but he was standing by the window now. As Naveed stared at the road with a melancholy look, Alice stopped pacing and took notice.

"I've talked enough about my worries. Want to tell me what's bothering you?" Alice asked.

Naveed turned away from the window. Alice stood in front of him with her arms folded. She blocked his path to the kitchen. Naveed disappeared and reappeared behind her, causing Alice to throw up her hands.

"Come on, Naveed, just tell me. You'll feel better," Alice said.

"Don't you have an interview?" Naveed asked as he opened the refrigerator.

Alice looked at her wristwatch. It was ten minutes to three. Alice could get to the museum just in time if she left now, or within seconds if she used Naveed's help. She looked at Naveed, calculating.

"Why are you squinting like that?" Naveed asked.

Instead of answering, Alice walked to the phone. She called the World Cultures Museum and gave her apologies. She could not picture working anywhere, but Many Treasures. She belonged on Magic Row.

When she hung up the phone, she could not stop smiling. Naveed, on the other hand, frowned.

"Didn't that job pay twice what you make now?" Naveed asked.

"It did, but I don't need the money. I'm happy right where I am," Alice said.

Naveed looked at his surroundings. He held his hands up, "You're happy with this?"

"I have friends and people who feel like family. I even have you," Alice said.

"As a captive," Naveed said under his breath. He clicked open a soda can and drank, afterwards adding, "You need a bigger TV."

Alice smiled. She grabbed her jacket and opened the front door. "Come on, let's go to Many Treasures, and tell them we're staying."

Naveed reluctantly transformed and followed her out of the building. The walk went quickly, and Alice was surprised to see Puck downstairs with Eric in Many Treasures. Eric was showing him how to ring up customers, though there weren't any in the store at the moment.

"Already got your hands on the cash?" Alice teased Puck.

He laughed, saying, "Promise not to take it, but not that I won't make it disappear." He waved a hand, and a dollar bill appeared in his palm.

"Puck, no magic!" Alice said. "Learn to do it the Untalented way."

"He did," Eric said. "I don't know many tricks, but I showed him the whole 'dollar between your knuckles trick,'" Eric said.

"Untalented *'magic'* is easy," Puck said. He looked at Alice curiously, adding, "What I want to know is how you made a blue charmed stone glow purple. That's the best trick I've heard all year."

Naveed jumped up onto the counter and looked at Alice too. She froze. The room went silent—or would have if it hadn't been interrupted by Eric's sneeze.

"I don't get it. You have a stone that changes colors? Is that a big deal?" Eric asked.

"The biggest. Charmed stones only react like that if they're near powerful and ancient magic," Puck said.

Alice looked at Naveed, who she swore was smiling. Powerful and ancient? That was Naveed. The charmed stone may have picked up something about his presence. That was a much better explanation than Alice being a witch. So much for that hope.

"Alice is powerful?" Eric couldn't have looked more skeptical if he was a full-fledged astronaut having a discussion with a flat-earther.

"I could be powerful," Alice said.

Puck scratched his head. "I don't know. Usually,

ancient magic is stored in things like a ring or a jewel of some sort."

"Or a necklace? Could a charmed stone detect another charmed stone?" Alice asked.

"Yeah, that might explain it, if the stone was holding an ancient spell," Puck said. He stood up, eagerly, "Why? Do you have one? Can I see it?"

"I'd show it to you if I knew where I put it. I haven't seen it in years. I'm going upstairs to have tea with Mrs. Kinjo." Alice said. She walked to the back of the shop.

Upstairs, a dozen photo albums sat open on the coffee table, all open to pictures of Alice. Further inside, Mrs. Kinjo could be heard speaking to someone. Alice followed the sound to the kitchen, where scattered photos and an old camera lay. Mrs. Kinjo was seated across from a woman whose back faced the door.

Alice recognized her by the flowery clothing style. "Belinda?" she asked.

"Good afternoon," Belinda turned around. She then turned back to sip her tea.

"There's a cup on the counter and plenty in the pot. Come sit with us, you'll find this fascinating," Mrs. Kinjo said.

"What's going on?" Alice asked.

She was too surprised to take anything to drink. Instead, she sat down beside Belinda and looked at her quizzically. Belinda set her teacup down.

"You're wondering what I'm doing here," Belinda said.

"I'm wondering a lot of things," Alice said.

Belinda quirked her head. "Like what?"

"Like how you knew the fire would be set to Merlin's Shadow," Alice said.

Belinda's eyebrows sank in confusion, then floated back up as the epiphany came to her. "My drawings. You saw that."

Mrs. Kinjo said, "You need not be alarmed by that. Belinda is a seer, my dear. I have always suspected such things to be true, and now I see it is."

Alice froze, looking between Mrs. Kinjo and Belinda. The way she was speaking was sure to make a witch suspect she was non-magical. Did Mrs. Kinjo not realize the danger in what she was saying? "Hamee," Alice began in a warning tone.

"It's all right," Belinda said. "I know she's not a witch, but I won't tell. I'm not quite sure what kind of a witch you are, Alice, but I do know you're different."

"What kind of a seer are you?" Alice asked. Her tone came off sharp, she knew it. But she couldn't help it if she sounded a little rude. Eric and Puck hadn't warned her that Mrs. Kinjo had company, which Eric most certainly would have done if he'd known Belinda were here. That meant Belinda has snuck into the apartment. Plus, she had drawn a fire before it had begun. And now she was looking at pictures of Alice. It was enough to arouse suspicions. Although Alice wasn't sure what accusation to make.

"I'm not actually a seer. It's my camera, which was spelled by a seer. It sees things in the past and future—sometimes. I can't predict when it will show me things. But, my Talent is my eye for detail. When the camera is showing something, I can use my powers to see what's there."

"Like you did with the charmed stone at the auction?" Alice asked.

"Exactly," Belinda said.

"So, what are you doing here?" Alice asked.

Belinda opened her purse and took out a magnifying glass. Like before, she whispered into the glass, and it fogged. This time, she handed the spelled lens to Alice.

"Go ahead, look at yourself in these old pictures."

"These are pictures you took of the photo album," Alice said, confused. Who would take a picture of a picture? It made no sense.

"This one's new. You can start here if you like." Belinda pointed to one she had taken the day of the auction at A Witch's Thrift Shop.

Alice had no idea why she was listening to Belinda or what to expect when she looked through the glass. She'd either see nothing or a clue she was sure she wasn't going to like. Her hand hovered over her own image. At first, it seemed blurred through the fog, but as the lens cleared, Alice saw a faint red glow around her neck.

Alice quickly looked at the pictures of the old album pictures Belinda had taken with her camera. There at Eric's graduation, there at her eighteenth birthday, there at their last Thanksgiving's meal, in all the pictures, Alice wore a charmed stone.

She looked up at Belinda. Belinda and Mrs. Kinjo were looking, not at her, but at her chest. She could see it now. The stone was not glowing at the moment, but it was there hanging around her neck. Alice jumped back, standing up so fast the chair crashed to the ground behind her.

"I've had this on me the whole time?" She asked.

"It must have masked itself through magic," Belinda said.

"What kind of magic? Charmed stones hold one spell, right? What kind of a spell is this?" Alice asked.

Belinda shook her head. "That's beyond me, but it doesn't seem like an ordinary stone. This could be ancient magic."

"Woah, cool!" said Puck. He and Eric had run upstairs, probably at the sound of the old wood chair falling overhead. Alice picked up the chair and set it straight again. She sat down, holding the stone as if she was mesmerized. They all were.

"What is that?" Eric asked, coming closer but still a safe three feet away.

Puck walked right up to it and stared wide-eyed. Even Naveed showed an interest, jumping up on the table so he could come face to face with the stone. Alice dropped it.

She sounded more than a little irritated as she said, "Apparently, none of us have any idea what this is or anything about it."

"That is untrue. We know it's from your parents, given to you by your mother, and that is has been with you since you can remember," Mrs. Kinjo said.

"Except I forgot about it, and it somehow went invisible while I was wearing it!" Alice said.

"You've been wearing it for years and no one noticed? That's amazing," Puck said.

"OK, a wizard is impressed by magic. Should I be worried?" Eric asked.

"It depends on if the magic is good or bad, and, as Alice pointed out, we don't know that," Belinda said.

"We need a powerful wizard who could identify such an ancient magic," Puck said.

"Do you know a wizard like that? Please say no," Eric said.

"As a matter of fact, we do," Alice said.

"Oh great," Eric made a vain attempt at a smile. "Who is it?"

Alice, Belinda, and Puck answered simultaneously, "Rhys Merlin."

TWENTY

Engagement Party

A lice had hoped to avoid Baz's engagement party, but no such luck. Rhys Merlin had taken one look at Alice's necklace and informed her that he would need time to investigate its origin. By 'time,' he had meant anywhere between "a single cycle of the moon to enough solar cycles for a lifetime."

If Alice wanted his most immediate and therefore, *'wildly incomplete'* version of his findings, she had to give Rhys at least to the end of the week. That meant, of course, that the first opportunity to meet for a discussion would be at the engagement celebration.

The invitation instantaneously transported Alice and Naveed to Baz's uncle, Perseus Delvaux's mansion. The combination of magical travel and the enchanting sight of the home stunned Alice. The tight bodice of her gown made breathing impossible after such a shock. Naveed had no such reaction. He immediately disappeared, reminding Alice that she'd once again forgotten to officially wish he would stop doing that.

Alice took a moment to recover, standing on the steps clutching the red stone at her exposed collar bone. Now she wished she had spent the money on a new coat. Her gold shawl was the fanciest covering she owned that matched with her gown. The gown itself was a modification of the prom dress Mrs. Kinjo had been kind enough to buy for Alice years ago as a graduation present. It had been expensive at the time but felt inadequate compared to the scene in front of her. The only valuable thing she was wearing was the red charmed stone, and she had no idea what that really cost.

Alice blinked. Her eyes were stinging from the contacts she wasn't used to wearing. She felt like a fraud — utterly unworthy to enter the mansion, which might have come from a catalog of fairy-tale castles. A fog dimmed the city in the background so that only the light visible poured out from rows of arched windows. The castle—as Alice was now committed to calling it—had several pointed rooftop sections that reminded Alice of stereotypical witch's hats. The most prominent of these topped the tall, cylindrical east and west towers. Alice shuddered, recalling a fight in Baz's mansion just a week ago.

Tonight was a happier occasion, though it had every chance of ending in a fight between the engaged couple. That depended on Alice's silence. It felt like lying, but she had decided to keep Tom and Titania's affair secret.

To be fair, Alice was already lying to everyone on Magic Row. Mrs. Kinjo had always said truths have a way of coming out. *Just not tonight,* Alice prayed. She took a deep breath and rang the doorbell.

The butler answered with a bow and offered to take her shawl, which she declined. He led her into a hall that looked fit for kings. Lit chandeliers hung from impossibly tall ceilings. Ornate entrées floated in fancy dishes offering themselves to guests, who stood on a marble floor discussing politics and their points of view on recent events.

Alice had never felt so alone among a group of people. She stood toward the entrance looking for a friendly or familiar face. Maybe she would stay in the front since Rhys seemed not to be here yet.

"Alice?" Baz took her by surprise, standing close behind her when she turned around. Titania was not with him, and though they were surrounded by a room full of people, Alice felt that she and Baz were alone. She blushed as Baz began with, "You look…" He stopped short of a compliment. If Baz was going for a dramatic pause, he lingered ten seconds too far.

"Nice?" Alice offered.

Baz straightened as if returning to his senses. "Yes. Have you come alone this evening?"

Alice leaned forward, looking past Baz's shoulder. "I was supposed to meet Rhys here."

"Oh?" Baz raised an eyebrow.

"As a friend," Alice added quickly. She didn't know why she was clarifying that. The sudden thought that Baz might see her and Rhys were a couple mortified her, not because Rhys wasn't still attractive in a mature way, but because he was so far from her type— her type apparently being Baz himself. Alice blushed.

A redness flushed over Baz's face, too. "No, no, you misunderstand my surprise. I was under the impression that Rhys was out of town."

"I heard my name, and I am here." Rhys Merlin called out from the doorway. He handed his patchwork coat to the doorman. His suit was a brown velvet that made Alice feel better about her repurposed prom dress. They could be misfits together. She smiled as he greeted her with a nod and a wink over his silver-rimmed glasses.

"Good to see your secret travels went well." Baz sounded like he felt slighted, or at least annoyed.

Rhys smiled wide, ignoring or perhaps forgiving Baz's incivility. He reached out and shook Baz's right hand with both of his own.

"Congratulations," Rhys said. Strangely, the word sounded more like heartfelt condolences.

Alice couldn't tell how Baz took it. His face was nothing but a puzzle to her most of the time. If there was a secret code for deciphering Baz's moods, she hadn't learned it yet. Alice added her congratulations, but she wasn't sure Baz had even heard.

Baz excused himself with a polite, "Thank you," and a less gracious, "Please don't take 'my mansion is your mansion' so literally this time Rhys." Baz took a step, then turned around, adding, "Miss Adelcraft?"

"Yes?" Alice asked, expecting a thank you.

But Baz replied, "Bewitching was the word I meant

to say." He turned around again, and this time disappeared into the crowd.

Rhys leaned toward Alice, saying, "My dear, you are blushing."

"Am I?" Alice said, too shocked to argue that she was not. Was she, though? Alice touched her cheeks, wondering— not for the first time— how Baz could have such an effect on her. She shook her head. Now was the time to analyze the stone, not her psyche.

"Can you tell what kind of magic was used on this?" Alice held up the necklace.

"Not here," Rhys said. He offered an arm. Alice took his offer and Rhys patted her forearm, smiling. "Hold tight," he said. Then he took a few steps toward the back yard, leading her outdoors and somehow onto a third story balcony.

"Woah," Alice said. She grabbed the railing, suddenly developing a whole new level to her fear of heights.

"So very sorry. Don't worry, your stomach will catch up with you eventually. When it does, try not to barf."

"Is this what Baz meant about making his mansion your own?" Alice said between shallow breaths.

Rhys waved his hand, gesturing to Alice's necklace and dismissing the idea at the same time. "I added a wing to his library to store my books. It's such a wonderfully designed library, I couldn't resist."

"You added a wing to another man's home?" Alice asked.

Rhys studied the stone around Alice's neck while

explaining, "I've added hidden places in nooks and crannies all through Urbana."

"Isn't doing that an invasion of people's privacy?"

"I respect everyone's right to privac— especially my own. Being a powerful person means that everyone wants your secret to success, especially any shortcuts to it. People study me, follow me, even try to spy on me. I need places no one knows to follow me."

"Baz knows about your hidden library," Alice pointed out.

"Baz will one day know all of my secrets," Rhys looked at Alice, dropping the necklace, he added, "Even the ones I keep for others."

Alice clutched the stone. She held it so tight her palm hurt. "You'd tell Baz about me?"

"You may need Baz to protect you."

"Why?" Alice asked.

Rhys pointed to her hand. "Remove that so I can get a better look."

Alice hesitated. She wanted an answer first, but she wasn't in a position to demand it. She did as she was told.

Or at least, she tried to unclasp the necklace. The moment she attempted to remove it, it disappeared. Alice gasped, but Rhys didn't seem startled.

"As I suspected, there is defensive magic in place should you try to remove it," Rhys said.

"Why would my parents give me a charmed stone I can't take off?" Alice asked.

"They obviously wanted to bind it to you," Rhys said.

"Is it binding my powers?" Alice asked.

Rhys patted Alice's arm and pointed to a table and chairs. Even the balcony furniture looked more expensive than what Alice could afford, a varnished teakwood and marble top mix. Rhys and Alice took seats opposite each other. Alice sank into the white cushion feeling all the comfort of the chair fading as Rhys's expression changed.

"This will be difficult for you to hear," Rhys said. Alice felt her heartbeat increasing. She didn't ask questions, just waited for Rhys to continue. "That is not a binding stone, it would have no effects on a witch's powers."

Alice felt her stomach turn. Whatever tiny bit of hope Alice had that she might be magical was gone. Worse, she'd just given her secret away. Rhys would surely guess from her question about binding that Alice had no powers in her grasp. Rather than looking like he would turn her in to any authority, Rhys looked at her with pity.

Alice exhaled, asking, "I'm really not a witch, am I? I don't have any magic."

Rhys quirked his head, his eyes telling her there was more to it than that. "You don't have powers, Alice. What you have is a destiny."

Alice shook her head. "I don't understand."

"There is very little magic in this world that can alter destiny. Usually, we have to trust events to work themselves out or our destiny changes in a moment, and we have to seize those opportunities that will set the course of our lives."

"You're saying this stone altered my destiny?"

"I'm not certain yet, but stones like these, they tend to do drastic things. If one is bound to you, you must be very, very special."

"I wish I was, but I don't feel that I am," Alice said.

"You shouldn't wish for a thing like that. Special isn't always good. If your own parents bound some magic to you, it's either to allow you to do some wonderful things or terrible ones."

"What things? What destiny am I supposed to fulfill?"

"Or not fulfill," Rhys said. He shrugged, adding, "I can only guess one thing."

Alice thought a moment and then put a hand to her forehead. *Of course. It was so obvious!* "I wasn't supposed to find Magic Row?"

"I think your parents never intended for you to know anything about witches."

"But why?"

"Perhaps to protect you or to protect them," Rhys said.

"You can't really think that. I'm not even capable of hurting them, and if I was, I wouldn't." Alice hadn't meant to raise her voice, but she was almost yelling at Rhys. She found herself on the edge of her chair, panting when she was done speaking. Rhys showed no reaction.

"I'm sure that's true," Rhys asked.

Alice's brow creased. There was something in the way Rhys said it. He was holding something back.

"What aren't you telling me?" Alice asked.

Rhys reached forward and put a hand on atop hers, "I don't know your parent reasons. Anything I say will only be guesses, but I promise I will investigate."

Alice relaxed. She nodded, saying, "Thank you, I—"

A door slammed shut, silencing Alice. Rhys put a finger to his lips. Then he waved a hand and disappeared from sight.

"Rhys?" Alice whispered.

Rhys's voice still coming from the chair made Alice flinch. "We're invisible. Stay quiet," Rhys said.

"The truth, Titania." A male voice came from inside the room adjacent to the balcony where Rhys and Alice sat. The voice sounded strong but raspy, like an elderly person.

The curtains were closed, so it didn't much matter that Alice and Rhys were invisible. The light from indoors flicked on. Alice could see two silhouettes inside.

"I already told Baz. I was just trying to help Mara-"

"Save it," the voice said. "It would be bad enough, Baz marrying a thief but an adulteress… I'm not sure I can stand for that."

"I never cheated on Baz!" Titania said.

"Never?" The voice was angry, "I hear reports otherwise from everywhere. People don't keep secrets on Magic Row, not even the secret of its existence these days."

"I didn't let that vandal into Magic Row. Everyone knows it was Ramsey," Titania pleaded.

"I mean that lawyer."

"He was never on Magic Row," Titania said.

Alice bit her lip. Tom had been on the magical street, but Titania wouldn't have known that. That was Alice's and Belinda's doing.

The man waved a hand. "It doesn't matter where you held your little rendezvous with an Untalented man —my god, a *married* Untalented man! There's no excuse for it, Titania. I won't have it in my family."

"What?" Titania's silhouette sank to sit on the edge of the bed.

The man's silhouetted moved to the door. "You will not marry my nephew. Baz will call off the engagement tomorrow," the man said.

"Baz would not do that to me," Titania said.

"Do you think it was his idea to marry you in the first place, you ridiculous girl? Baz will do what I say, as he has always done. He knows his duty as a Delvaux. I thought the Knights shared the same sense of honor. I was gravely mistaken." The man's silhouette disappeared out the door.

Titania flung herself onto the bed, wailing in great, heaving sobs. Instinctively, Alice stood. She might have walked right inside to console Titania, except that a hand snaked around her arm and pulled her back. One nausea-inducing second later, Alice doubled over fresh grass, grasping a juniper tree and dry-heaving.

"Goodness, you do have a reaction to magical travel, don't you?" Rhys asked.

"Thanks for the warning!" Alice said.

Rhys ignored her. "Do me a favor and forget the conversation you just saw."

"We shouldn't have been eavesdropping," Alice admitted once she regained her composure.

Rhys smiled, "Well, that is the problem with secret hiding places. Sometimes you overhear a thing or two."

"What happened to privacy?" Alice asked.

Rhys tapped his nose with his index finger. "I do keep everyone's secrets."

"Then how did Baz's uncle find out?" Alice asked.

"Baz and Perseus together own all of Magic Row, except for Many Treasures. If Perseus had anything to do with it, he'll own that soon, too, Alice. You think there's anything that they don't find out eventually?"

"Secrets have a way of coming out." Alice repeated Mrs. Kinjo's sentiment. She put a hand to her forehead. "Oh no, poor Baz," Alice said.

"I wouldn't feel too sorry for him," Rhys said.

"Do you think he'll be heartbroken? And Titania, will she be OK?" Alice asked.

"You are a sweet girl," Rhys said. Then he winked and pointed to a tree in the far corner of the yard. "Now go cheer up your cat."

Alice walked past the row of junipers and found Naveed sulking on the other side of a hedgerow, at the entrance of what looked like a maze. There was a bench there and he was sitting on it, looking down.

"Are you all right?" Alice asked.

He looked up at her with the moonlight reflecting in his black eyes, and Alice could see they were watery. He transformed into his jinn form, midnight blue in the dim light of the garden. Alice walked over to him. He turned his face away because, Alice imagined, he didn't want her to see the tear rolling down his cheek.

"You still don't want to talk about it?" Alice asked.

"No," Naveed said.

"All right." For the first time in days, Alice didn't argue. She turned around to leave.

Naveed sighed, a deep, dramatic, deafening sigh that made it obvious he wanted to get something off his massive chest.

Alice turned back and crossed her arms. "Do you want me to make it a command that you tell me what has you down?"

Now Naveed looked her in the eyes. Like his usual stubborn self, he asked, "Is it a command?"

Alice almost dropped the whole conversation, but she could see what Naveed was doing. He wanted to tell her, but his pride wouldn't let him. If Alice made it a command, he could deny that he wanted to open up. And Naveed said humans had the fragile egos. Fine. If he needed it to be a command, Alice would make it one.

"Yes," Alice said.

Naveed scooted over, allowing Alice a space on the bench. She sat next to him and waited patiently. Naveed seemed to struggle for words.

She helped him out. "Is this about Hex?"

He looked at her horrified as if Alice had been reading his most private thoughts. Alice explained, "You kept disappearing lately and Puck said he saw you and Hex talking. When Hex ran away from you at the car repair shop, I figured that's why you've been disappeared—to see Hex."

Naveed nodded. "I've tried everything, but she won't let me near her."

"Have you tried being nice and not all moody and growling."

Naveed gave her a displeased look. "I've tried approaching her kindly several times, but she won't let me talk. She pushes me away, she even uses her magic on me to turn me back into a cat."

Alice tried to imagine Hex in jinn-form but had no reference point for her eyes or skin or hair color. The only thing she could picture was Hex's eyes. Naveed's stayed the same in cat form, so Alice imagined Hex's did, too. Even the gold eyes Alice saw in her mind had no face to go with it. "What does Hex look like in jinn form?" Alice asked.

Naveed looked up at the stars. "She's the most beautiful sight in all of creation," Naveed said. Then he blinked and looked at Alice. "I mean, she's OK."

Alice rolled her eyes, "Oh yeah, tell her she's OK. Any woman would fall for that."

Naveed frowned. "I have told her she is beautiful."

"And?" Alice asked.

"She says beauty is in the heart—and mine is the ugliest she's ever seen."

"She said that?"

Naveed looked at Alice from the corner of his eye and said, "Yes."

"Really?" Alice raised an eyebrow.

"She said I shouldn't talk to her until I change it." He insisted.

"She wants you to have a change of heart. What

about, I wonder?" Alice asked. She could guess. Naveed only had a maximum of two subjects he ever discussed: Hex and humanity. Mostly hexing humanity and how he would go about it.

Hex, the female jinn, he quite obviously loved. The other one, he hated.

"Hex feels humans are 'precious,' in need of our care." Naveed's lip curled.

"And you think we should all be destroyed," Alice said. She didn't bother to make it a question. She knew how Naveed felt. He neither confirmed or denied the sentiment. "If you want my opinion, which of course you don't, all you have to do is work on your communication skills."

He raised an eyebrow. "How will that help?"

"You'll be able to tell her how you really feel about humans, for one."

"She knows how I really feel about humans. That is the entire problem."

Naveed might have fooled Hex; he might have even fooled himself, but Alice saw through him. She had seen the tears when Naveed's previous master had died. Alice knew a farce when she saw one.

She'd seen him upset about his last master's death. Alice knew he had taken a liking to the Willows and to Puck. He even seemed to care for Alice, as much as he tried to hide it.

"I don't think you know how you feel about humans, Naveed. When you're ready to figure it out, I'm sure she'll be willing to listen. And I will be, too." Alice patted Naveed's knee, then stood and left him with his mouth agape, watching her leave the maze.

As Alice turned the corner of the hedges, she saw a tall woman with bronze skin and sparkling eyes watching her approach. Alice was struck by the sight, not just because she wasn't expecting to see anyone. It wasn't even because the woman was incredibly beautiful—like Alice's idea of what Nefertiti or a Cleopatra might have looked like — but because the eyes reminded Alice of Hex's brilliant gold orbs. The woman gave Alice a silent nod, then turned and walked into the hedges, vanishing as she went.

Alice looked back at the mansion. Past the glass sliding doors, Liza was dancing with her husband. Ron flirted with a small group of very attractive witches. Celeste chatted in a circle with a small group of mages, who were nodding as if in agreement. Belinda was taking pictures. Alice felt the glimmer of hope fade when she saw it.

All of Rhys's talk about destinies had Alice wondering if the damage that would come tomorrow and this picture of a happy community would change. Titania and Tom's affair would be revealed, and Liza's heart would be broken. But Ron might have the chance to mend it. Baz might be devastated, or he might be relieved. Who knew what was in their destiny?

What fate did Alice have that was so terrible her parents had to try to change it? She should never have set foot in Magic Row, but now that she had, she cared about the people who belonged to that street. Alice may not have magic, but she did not have to be a mage to know that real magic was in the friendships she had made. Through Liza, Hazel, Zade, Puck, Vestra, Celeste, and all the others, Alice had become a part of this magical community. She would do whatever she could to protect her friends—even if the day would come when she would have to leave them...and forget.

The people of Magic Row were worth facing any hex or challenge Alice's destiny had in store.

Epilogue

The evening did not end there. To all the guests, including Alice, it appeared that the party lasted only until the last couple straggled out at midnight. But the strike of the clock was not how the night concluded. It ended as the worst nightmares do: with a death.

The Story Continues...

Read about a death at Delvaux's Mansion in Book 3: Wicked Wish Lists.

Go to astoriawright.com for more info on this series and others by the author.